Hummingbirds, Pennies, and Hope

Hummingbirds, Pennies, and Hope

Jeanne Lemmon Skinner

BALBOA.
PRESS
A DIVISION OF HAY HOUSE

Balboa Press books may be ordered through booksellers or by contacting:

Balboa Press
A Division of Hay House
1663 Liberty Drive
Bloomington, IN 47403
www.balboapress.com
1-(877) 407-4847

Library of Congress Control Number: 2012904067

ISBN: 978-1-4525-4836-4 (sc)
ISBN: 978-1-4525-4837-1 (hc)
ISBN: 978-1-4525-4835-7 (e)

Printed in the United States of America

Balboa Press rev. date: 3/26/2012

Dedicated to my daughter, Jill, and friend, Mary, who were also students of our gifted teacher, Doreen Virtue.

Chapter 1

"This is a research paper I think you'll actually enjoy," said Ms. Peters as she stood before the class and smiled at her humor. As expected, her English class responded with a loud groan. "You will be selecting a topic that interests you. Think of it as an opportunity to learn about something new and exciting; I am emphasizing the word 'new.' I will not read fifty papers about the history of professional football. Your topics are due Friday, and I reserve the right to veto any topic." The bell rang, and Ms. Peters was quickly surrounded by questioning students.

Frustrated with another assignment, Anna pushed past the students and entered the crowded hallway. *Another research paper! Doesn't she get tired of grading? I have a paper due for Mr. Coates next week on the survivors of the Holocaust. I just don't have the time or the energy to write another paper,* thought Anna as she walked to her locker.

"Wait up!" called Maddie, Anna's best friend. She was on her way to audition for the upcoming fall play, *The Crucible,* and was visibly anxious. "Wish me luck," she said as she clutched the script.

"I don't know why you're so nervous. You're great. You're always great, but if saying good luck makes you feel better, good luck! We read one of the scenes from *The Crucible* in drama class, and Mr. Biggs explained the symbolism. We all wanted to read more, but he said we had to try out in order to find out what happens. I wish I could try out just to see how it ends," Anna said as she tossed most of her books into her locker.

"He's good at giving teasers. Hopefully, you'll be in the spring musical. It'll be even more fun than this. You still plan to be on the stage crew for the play, don't you?" Maddie asked anxiously.

Brushing her hair away from her eyes, Anna said, "It depends on how Grandma is doing, but I think I'll be able to help with costumes and makeup. That way I can earn Thespian points, and we'll still be together."

"We're stuck together like peanut butter and jelly, as your grandmother says. You can't have one without the other. I'll call you later and give you all the details from tryouts," Maddie promised.

Anna watched her friend walk away. Maddie was pretty and talented, a winning combination that made her one of the most popular girls in school. She was tall and blonde, and she walked with the grace of a dancer. As she passed a group of boys, they all turned and smiled. Thom Deal wished her good luck on the tryouts, and his whole face smiled when he spoke. Thom had liked Maddie since freshman year. Unfortunately for Thom, Maddie considered him just a friend and they had never been on a date.

Anna gathered her things and headed for home. She was glad that she could walk to school. It gave her time to unwind, and on beautiful days like today, she could enjoy being outside. She loved the fall. She kicked the brightly colored leaves as she walked. A shower of crimson and orange surrounded her feet.

As Anna approached the library, she saw that the sun had illuminated the fountain in the courtyard. The sparkling water splashed happily from the top of the three tiers to the bottom. Yellow mums had been planted at the fountain's base, and the whole area had a golden glow. *I think I'll run in and see if I can find something to research,* thought Anna. *At the moment, nothing sounds very interesting except a nice, warm chocolate brownie dripping with chocolate icing.*

As she walked past the teen section in the library, Anna stopped to see what was new. *More vampire books? I don't get it! What's with this vampire craze? I would never want to be a vampire; I enjoy food too much. No way would I exchange eating chocolate for drinking blood!* Anna knew what a few people were researching, but nothing sounded very exciting. She wanted something new and unique.

She wandered into the hobby and craft section because Sara Little said she was going to research how to make paper. Anna looked at various books, but she wasn't very artsy, and she was sure Ms. Peters would expect her to actually produce an example of what she had researched. Sara would make her own paper and then do something creative with it, making it look incredible. *I can't see myself creating anything I'd want to share except a large veggie pizza with extra cheese,* she thought as her hunger announced itself again.

The next section was self-help books. There were some interesting topics, but nothing drew Anna in. *Nope, nothing here,* she thought, beginning to feel discouraged. The next aisle held spiritual books, and Anna thought of all the books in her grandmother's book case at home. *Grandma loves these books. Hmm, this might be interesting, a book about communicating with angels. I wonder if Ms. Peters will approve it. I bet no one else will choose this. Hey, as long as I can write five pages about it, I'm good.* Anna glanced at her watch and knew she had to hurry. Mom would have to leave soon to get to the shop, and she was needed to stay with Grandma. Anna quickly checked out the angel book and headed home in the fall sunshine.

"Hi! I'm home!" Anna shouted as she opened the front door. She walked into the kitchen, but no one was there. *They must be outside,* she thought. The glass doors that led to the patio were open and the fresh fall air filled the room. She could see her mother and grandmother sitting in the yard by the flower garden; their chairs were surrounded by leaves, and they were peeling apples. She wondered if she'd have time to rake after dinner. Raking leaves was one of Anna's favorite fall activities. She felt sorry for people who didn't get to experience it. She cheerfully crossed the yard and picked up a bouquet of colorful leaves and pretended they were a bridal bouquet.

"Hey, you two! Are we going to have apple pie?" Anna asked excitedly.

"Apple crisp tonight," her grandmother, Ellen, said with a gentle smile. "I still have energy for a few things, and peeling these apples makes me feel useful. Your mom bought a whole basket at the farmers market. Feel free to join me in peeling them."

"I think we need to go inside now, Mom," said Karen, Anna's mother. "It's gotten cool since the sun left the yard. The meatloaf and potatoes should be ready soon. Maybe you could make the apple crisp for dessert tonight, Anna." Karen took the bowl of apples from her mother and handed them to Anna. She then gently helped her mother rise from the chair. "It's too difficult to use the walker in the grass, but we took our time and made it," she said to Anna. Turning to her mother she said, "Take hold of Anna's arm, Mom. That will give you more support."

The three Williams women slowly made it into the house. A stranger could tell they were related because they looked so much alike. Even their voices were similar. Their most striking features were green eyes and pale skin. Freckles were a nuisance for each of them, and each had spent hours either trying to prevent them or hide them. Cancer was taking Ellen Williams from her daughter and granddaughter, but she was trying to find joy in every day she had left. Spending time in the yard surrounded by nature's beauty brought her much pleasure. She had spent many hours working in her own flower beds and then later her daughter's. Gardening had been one of her passions. Ellen was not looking forward to winter and was determined to hold on to the fall as long as she could.

"Well, it looks like you can take charge now, Anna. Grandma's medicine is right here. I'll be home about ten. Call if you need me," said Karen as she picked up her keys.

"Okay, Mom. We'll be fine. The apple crisp will be waiting for you when you get home," Anna said, and then she helped her grandmother get comfortable in a chair.

"Grandma, I'll get the topping made for the crisp while the meatloaf finishes baking. You sure peeled a lot of apples today. "

"Just put a little sugar on them and put them in freezer bags. That way they'll be ready for your next crisp or pie. I think I'll rest here in my chair while you work. All that fresh air has made me tired." Grandma smiled as she closed her tired eyes.

"Oh, dear Lord, please be with my grandma. I love her so much. I don't want to lose her. We could sure use a miracle, if you still do that. She is getting worse each week." Anna prayed as she worked butter into the brown sugar and oats.

The timer beeped, indicating that the meatloaf was done. Anna quietly got dinner on the table and went to wake her grandmother. "Grandma, dinner's ready," she said as she gently shook her. Anna tried again, but her grandmother could not be awakened.

Chapter 2

"I can't believe she's gone. We were supposed to have more time. She was just resting before dinner, and then ..." Anna didn't think she could cry anymore; that's all she had done for three days. She was very thankful that Maddie had come home with her after the memorial service.

"Let's get something to eat. You really need something in your stomach. It will help you feel better," said Maddie.

The house was filled with family and friends, and Karen was busy arranging food platters and talking with people. Anna knew her mother was aching like she was, but she had things to take care of before she could sit and grieve. The girls took their food outside and sat by what her grandmother called the "angel garden." She had named it in honor of the angel statue that adorned the bed. The red knockout roses were still blooming, along with lavender and black-eyed susans. Karen had planted yellow and amber colored mums a few weeks ago, and the garden looked lovely.

"Grandma loved our yard as much as her own. She was always doing something out here," Anna said as she gazed at the flowers. "When she lost her strength, she would just sit here by the angel garden and breathe in its beauty. She said she wanted to spend as many of her last days as possible communing with nature. She would bring her journal with her and write. I asked her what she wrote about, and she simply said, 'Life.' She encouraged me to keep a journal, but I told her I wasn't much of a writer. She laughed and said that the beauty of keeping a journal was that it was personal. 'It's your thoughts, feelings, and ideas that no one will grade or even comment on. I know whatever I write is just for me. It helps me keep things in perspective if I write it down,' she would say. She was really a special person," Anna said proudly.

"I know. I loved her too," Maddie said softly, "Remember when we super glued ourselves together?" Both girls laughed, remembering how they had purposely glued their hands together so Maddie wouldn't have to go home.

"Grandma was frantic trying to unstick us! She called three people before she learned how to get us free. It's a good thing there was nail polish remover in the house. I don't think she could have held up much longer. As I think back, she didn't babysit us for quite a while after that," Anna said. It felt good to remember the fun times. The girls sat in comfortable silence, enjoying the beautiful fall day and thinking about Anna's grandmother.

"I bet I missed a lot at school this week. I know something is due for Ms. Peters on Monday. What is it?" asked Anna.

"We need to bring resource material to class for our research projects. We turned in our topics yesterday. Ms. Peters said to bring three resources, and we can have class time to read and take notes. Some of the topics sound really interesting. I'm going to like presentation day. Are you still thinking about researching angels?"

"Yes. I got one book at the library, and Grandma has two bookcases full of books. There has to be at least two about angels in there. What topic did you finally decide to research?"

"McCarthyism. Mr. Biggs told us that Arthur Miller wrote *The Crucible* as an allegory to the Salem Witch Trials. I want to learn more about Senator McCarthy and why people here in the United States were so afraid of Communism. It was called the Red Scare," said Maddie knowingly as if she were about to teach.

"I don't understand Communism," confessed Anna. "All I know is that it is the type of government that China has, and people don't have much freedom."

"I don't know why this happened, but during the 1950s, a person in the United States could be arrested or lose his job if he was thought to be a Communist. Mr. Biggs said that Arthur Miller was questioned about his political beliefs by the McCarthy committee, and so were a lot of other people in the theater business. It was a modern-day witch hunt, only Senator McCarthy was looking for Communists instead of witches," said "Professor" Maddie in a very serious tone of voice.

"I'm impressed. You seem to know a lot already. Speaking of *The Crucible*, do rehearsals begin on Monday?"

"Yeah. It's really going to be fun. I think you would have made it if you had been able to try out," Maddie said, and then added, "It would be more fun if you were in it too."

"Thanks, but I needed to be here for Grandma," Anna paused before continuing. "The doctor thought she had at least three more months. He was wrong about that. Mom said she is glad Grandma's last day was spent by the garden instead of in a hospital bed. I know she's right, but ..." Anna's voice faltered. She swallowed, and then she spoke. "I think it is great you're playing Elizabeth Proctor. Did Alison Bates make it? She was awesome when she read in drama class."

"Yeah, she made it. She's pretty good," Maddie said begrudgingly.

"You are too funny," Anna said laughing. "I can't believe you haven't gotten over her going out with Pete Saunders. You dumped him! What did you expect?"

"I just think if she had really been my friend she wouldn't have been so quick to rush in and grab him. Who knows, we might have gotten back together," Maddie said, trying to defend herself.

"You dumped Pete so you could go out with Will! Remember? Pete only went out with Alison to get back at you! Everyone knew it," Anna shook her head and continued. "You are truly crazy, but I love you anyway." Anna was so thankful that Maddie was with her and helping her reenter into their world of teenage drama. Being Maddie's friend meant there was always some event to prepare for or some crisis to live through, and right now she welcomed it. She wanted her chest to stop hurting, and she wanted to laugh and feel normal again.

Anna knew she had been outside long enough, so she and Maddie returned to the house. People were beginning to leave, and both girls started clearing the table and putting things away. There was enough food left for a week. It was nice that it was Saturday, and they could sleep in the next day.

After everyone left, Anna and her mother collapsed on the couch. "I think Mom would have been pleased with the service," said Karen. "I wonder if she was here today."

"Are you kidding?" asked Anna uncertainly.

"No, I'm quite serious. From what I have read, some deceased do attend their funerals," replied Karen thoughtfully.

"How would anyone know that?"

"Because there are people who have the ability to see the deceased. I've read books about it. You believe the spirit lives on after the body dies, right?" asked Karen.

"Yes," answered Anna cautiously.

"So, the spirit can visit just about anywhere it wants to, I guess. I read that many deceased loved ones linger around their family members for a while, trying to comfort them from the other side. That makes sense to me. I read about people who knew they were going to die, and they told their loved ones to watch for a sign that would indicate they were still with them," explained Karen.

"That is pretty amazing. Is that stuff in Grandma's books?" asked Anna as she reached for the cookie plate on the coffee table.

"Yes. Try the coconut ones; they're really good," Karen said glancing at the cookies. "Grandma read many spiritual books. I'm not sure how many she has."

"Did Grandma give you a sign to watch for?"

"No. We didn't even talk about it. I think I just knew I would know when she was around," Karen said softly with tears in her eyes.

Anna waited a few minutes and asked, "Would it be all right if I read some of her books? I'd like to use them for my English class. I decided to research angels," Anna said as she looked at her mother for a reaction.

Karen titled her head and gave Anna a curious look. "Why did you choose angels?"

"To be honest, I couldn't think of anything, and then I saw this book about angels, and I knew you and Grandma had books here at home. I thought it would be an easy project," Anna admitted and avoided her mother's eyes.

"I am sure your teacher didn't say choose what is easiest to research, but I don't think you'll be sorry you chose angels. There is a lot to learn. Would you like to look at some of Grandma's books now? I think I would. It might help me feel close to her," Karen said sadly.

"Let's go, Mom," Anna said as she pulled her mother to her feet. They quietly and reverently walked into what had been Grandma's room for the last six months. It felt uncomfortable knowing she wouldn't be there anymore. Sinking into the soft blue carpet in front of the bookcase, Karen began telling Anna about some of the authors and a little bit about the books. On the bottom shelf, they found Grandma's journals. Lying across the top of the journals was an envelope with Anna's name on it. Anna picked it up with quivering hands, carefully took the letter out, and began to read.

My dearest Anna,

I don't have the words to express how much I have enjoyed being your grandmother. I never got tired of hearing the word "Grandma." I am sorry I will not be attending your graduation, wedding, and other special occasions in person, but I will be there in spirit. Look for me. I will try my best to leave you a sign.

I am so glad Karen has you. If you can, encourage her to give that nice man Dan a chance. I have a good feeling about him. She shouldn't spend all her time at the flower shop.

I hope, in time, you will want to read some of my books. These books have brought me great comfort over the years, particularly after your grandfather passed away. Your grandpa did visit me from the other side, so I know it is possible for me to do the same. I believe the deceased can hear us call to them in prayer, so give it a try. I am confident I will be able to hear you.

You and your mother have been my greatest joy. You both filled the void that was left when Ed died. Thank you for your love. I know your life will be one of giving and receiving love. You already seem to understand that the more one gives, the more one receives.

Please feel free to read my journals that you always seemed so curious about. There are things in there that you will find both interesting and surprising. Take care of your mother, and remember that I am not far away. I am just on the other side.

Much love,
Grandma

Anna and Karen were smiling as tears ran down their cheeks.

Chapter 3

Karen had gone to bed, but Anna could hear her talking on the phone to Dan. He had been a great help this week. He had been there to help make the funeral arrangements and get the house ready for all the people who came after the service. Anna liked him, but she wasn't eager for him to become a part of their family. She didn't want to think about her mother getting married for a while. They got along great the way they were. It would be nice if things could stay the same until Anna graduated. She knew her mom was hesitant to marry, but after Anna was away at college, Anna thought her mother just might rethink her position on marriage. It was obvious how Dan felt about Karen, so Anna would be happy for her mother if that was what the future held for them; just not now.

Anna couldn't settle her mind long enough to allow for sleep. Her mind jumped from one topic to the next. She knew she wouldn't settle down until she read one of her grandmother's journals. She quietly got out of bed and returned to her grandmother's room. Anna pulled a blue journal off the shelf and began to read.

May 10
Karen wants me to go to an angel workshop with her. Ed thinks it's crazy. I am sure our

pastor would agree. I don't understand why the New Age Movement has people so upset. I guess I'll have to read Mary Matson's book. Ed says that's all I do, read and gardening.

May 15

I'm going to go. It's important to Karen, because she is really struggling with her divorce. If talking to angels helps her then I'm all for it. I started reading Mary Matson's book about angels. They seem to be a part of this spiritual craze. My friend Donna is into angels. She has a collection of them. She said she was raised fearing God, and all her pastor talked about was sin. When she discovered angels, she discovered God's love. She left her church and joined our church. That's where I met her. She said she is a strong believer that angels can help us. Donna told me that since she started asking her angels to help her find the things she misplaced, her days are a lot smoother. (She does lose things a lot.) I am going to try to communicate with my angels tonight. I'm going to try something I read in Mary's book.

May 16

I still can't believe this. I prayed and asked my angels to let me know they were with me by sending me a sign. I asked them to have someone call me that I had not heard from in a long time. This morning, Vicki called me. She said she just couldn't get me off her mind and had to call. I haven't talked to Vicki in almost a year! Ed

said it is a coincidence. I know it was my angels
letting me know they are with me.

Anna was in awe. She wondered if that would work for her
too. She could ask for a phone call, or maybe something else.
A penny, that's it; I'll ask my angels to leave me a penny. Anna
remembered her mom talking about finding pennies when she
had gone to the angel workshop. Anna was only eight years old
at the time, but she remembered the story about the pennies. She
prayed before she went to sleep and asked her angels to leave her
a penny.

Sunday was another beautiful day. Anna and her mother
attended church and Anna knew she had to get started on all
the homework that had piled up. She decided to take her history
book outside to read so she could enjoy the weather. As she was
walking through the grass, something shiny caught her eye. She
reached down and picked up a penny. "No way!" she shouted. She
sat down by the angel garden and stared at the statue. "I think
one of your friends left me this," she said to the statue and held
it for the statue to see. *I need to tell Mom*, Anna thought, and she
headed for the house.

Karen had done the laundry and decided go back to her
mother's room and look through her books. She had been
considering adding a new area to her flower shop, and she wanted
to make it something special. Her mother had loved books and
gardening. *Why not carry some spiritual books?* She thought. She
certainly knew people who said they felt closest to God when
they were working in their yards. A couple of her mother's friends
had meditation gardens similar to their angel garden. *That's what
I'll do; I'll carry books that tell how to establish a meditation garden, as well
as some books about meditating. I'll sell angel statues, and perhaps I could get
an angel fountain for the center of the ro—*

"Mom? Are you all right?" Anna found her mother sitting so still that it concerned her.

"Yes, I'm fine. I was just thinking about the shop. I have what I think is a great idea, and it was inspired by your grandmother," Karen said excitedly as she shared her thoughts.

"It's perfect. Grandma would have loved it."

"I think so too. You know Grandma bought me the angel we have in the garden. She said it would remind me of the wonderful time we had together at the angel workshop."

"I would like to hear more about the workshop. Neither of you ever said much about it."

"You were too little when we went. I guess it was something we kept between us.

Your grandfather thought it was a bunch of nonsense at first, but even he came around."

"What happened?" Anna asked as she grabbed a pillow and sat on the floor next to her mom's chair.

"Well, when we came back, we were both all excited about what we had seen and done and could hardly wait to tell people about it. Grandma's neighbor, Donna, was on vacation when we returned from our trip, so Grandma had to wait two long weeks for her. Meanwhile, Grandma told Grandpa everything. He prided himself in being open-minded, but he was having difficulty believing that people could see and communicate with angels. When she told him about channeling, he almost lost it." Karen laughed remembering. "He thought we had spent a lot of money to spend a week with a bunch of spiritual lunatics."

"Channeling?"

"Channeling is what a person does when he or she communicates with the deceased. The person who is channeling receives a message and then relays it to another person."

"People at this angel workshop did that?" asked Anna with a look of disbelief.

"Yes. I met a lady who had been a medium for five years and was attending the workshop to learn about angels. So, in other words, she was a professional at channeling. People came to her in order to talk to their loved ones who had passed over. I wasn't much of a believer in this until it actually happened to me."

Anna was mute as she stared at her mom.

"Let's get back to your grandfather. He was an intelligent man, and like your grandmother, he loved to read. He started researching the topic of séances and people who said they could talk to the dead. He was surprised to learn that the idea of talking to the deceased goes back hundreds of years. He also read stories about the deceased sending messages through music, scents, and even appearances. He wasn't convinced, but he agreed it could be possible.

"Donna finally returned. You can imagine the marathon conversation they must have had," Karen said with a chuckle. "Donna had read Mary Matson's book while on vacation, so she wasn't surprised by what Grandma told her. However, she was surprised to learn that your grandmother had been able to communicate with deceased loved ones at the workshop. You see, all day long for five days, we would find a partner and listen for messages from the other person's angels or their deceased loved ones," explained Karen.

"You both did this?" asked Anna with wide eyes.

"Everyone did it. It didn't feel strange at the time, but as I talk about it, I know that's how it must sound."

"Did you talk to dead people?" Anna whispered, clutching the pillow tightly to her chest.

"Yes, I did. Almost everyone there did. It wasn't scary. It was broad daylight. The sun filled the room; there were no candles or chanting. This wasn't a séance or a séance-like atmosphere."

"How did you do it?" Anna asked as she continued to squeeze the pillow for emotional support. *Who is this woman who calls herself my mother?* She wondered.

"Mary, our teacher, led us. We always prayed before we did anything. So we'd pray and then ask something about our partner. We would look to see if we saw anything around our partner, like colors or people."

"Mom, this is creepy."

"It wasn't creepy at all. It was wonderful to be able to know something or see something that helped my partner."

"Give me an example," requested Anna.

"Okay. We were told to look for deceased loved ones. I took my partner's hands and prayed to be able to see something that would help her. I had my eyes closed, but in my mind I clearly saw a man wearing a white minister's collar and a cross. It's like when you have a dream and you see something in your mind, only I was wide awake and holding someone hands. I dropped her hands and told her what I saw. She smiled and calmly said, 'That's my father. He was a Baptist minister. Do you see anything else?' I don't know how I did it, but I picked up her hands and tried again. Since she was so matter of fact about what was happening, and I just went along with her. I was surprised when I saw a big, white cat. I told her, and she nodded her head and said, 'Oh, that's Fluffy. My dad loved that cat.' This total stranger beamed at me because of what I had been able to tell her. I don't know how to explain where the information came from, except that I must have had angelic help."

"I think I would have fainted," said Anna.

"No, you wouldn't have. I know it doesn't sound natural, but it was natural for the people at the workshop. It was an experience that I probably won't ever have again, and it was awesome."

"Did that man you saw say anything?"

"No, I just saw him."

The conversation was interrupted by the phone ringing. Karen went to answer and returned. "It's your father. He wants to talk to you."

"I don't want to talk to him. Why didn't you tell him I wasn't here?" Anna said irritated.

"Because you are here," Karen said firmly. "Now go talk to him."

"Hello," greeted Anna in a flat voice.

"Hi, Anna, how are you doing? I thought of you and your mother yesterday. Was the service nice?"

"You should have come," Anna said sulkily.

"Honey, it would have been uncomfortable with me there," answered her father.

"It wouldn't have been uncomfortable for me," said Anna, wanting her father to know her displeasure.

"I'm sorry, Anna, I just couldn't. I did send flowers, you know," said Anna's father defensively.

That was easier than coming, wasn't it, Dad? thought Anna. She said, "Yes, Dad, you did."

"Ellen was a great lady and always treated me like a son, but divorce does change things. I assume your mother's friend, Dan, was there, so I wasn't needed."

What's that about? Dad's been married for three years, and he couldn't come because Mom has another man in her life? What a lame excuse. I could have used his support, Anna thought, feeling both angry and hurt.

"Okay, well the main reason I called was to tell you I have great news. We are moving back to Sweet Grove. Isn't that great?"

"You are? Why?" Anna asked totally surprised.

"The company needs me in Sweet Grove. I'm glad I'll be closer to you. I've missed a lot being three hours away."

"What does Mark think about moving here? I sure wouldn't want to change high schools," Anna said, wondering how this must be affecting her stepbrother.

"He is not happy about it, but I have to go where the company needs me. I know I can count on you to introduce him to some people. We won't move until after his football season is over, so that helps a little."

"What about Lauren? What does she think?"

"She isn't very happy either, but she can always find a job as a pharmacist. She hates to leave our house, but we'll find something nice in Sweet Grove. I have a realtor looking around for us. We're coming up next weekend to start looking. Would you like to look with us?"

"I don't think that would be a good idea, Dad. I can just see Lauren's face if I showed up. I seem to bring a cloud with me, and I wouldn't want to dampen her house-hunting enthusiasm. Besides, I have to work."

"Now, Anna, Lauren likes you. You need to be willing to give her a chance."

"Whatever, Dad," responded Anna sarcastically. She thought about all the chances she had given Lauren over the last three years. There was no possibility of them getting along. They simply didn't like each other.

"You can at least meet us for dinner. It would mean a lot to Mark. He is very nervous about this move."

"I'll try, Dad. Mom really needs me at the shop. I'll let you know."

"Anna, I want to see you, so you need to arrange your schedule in order to have dinner with us. This is an order, not a request."

"Okay, Dad." Anna knew when she was beaten. Her dad had given up on the every-other-weekend visits when Grandma moved in, so she knew she would now have to start seeing him and his other family again.

"We'll pick you up at 6:30 p.m. I'm looking forward to living closer to you. And, Anna, I'm really sorry about your grandmother. She was a great lady, and I know how much you'll miss her."

"Thanks, Dad. I'll see you Saturday." Anna hung up the phone filled with a variety of emotions. Mark Green moving to her town and going to her school; her wicked stepmother living nearby; things just keep getting worse. She was doomed. Poor, Mom; how was she going to feel about this? Dad living in Cincinnati had been good as far as her mom was concerned. At least she had Dan in her life now, but she'd have to see Anna's dad and Lauren from time to time. This couldn't be good.

Anna looked at the clock and knew she had to get some of her schoolwork done.

I don't have time to worry about Dad and his family, she thought, and she reached her hand into her pocket and pulled out her penny. She hadn't told her mom about finding it. That was the reason she had come inside. *I'll tell her later. I have to take books to school tomorrow for research, so I'd better look for some, and then I'll read my history.*

Anna went to her grandmother's room and started looking through her books. She knew there had to be a background section about her topic. That wouldn't be a problem. She could write about how the Bible, Torah, and Koran all mention angels. She could mention the angel Gabriel telling Mary she'd have a son, and she had just read about the angel Moroni. She hadn't known where the word Mormons had come from. Now she knew the story of John Smith receiving sacred writings from an angel named Moroni and starting the Church of Jesus Christ of the Latter-day Saints. That would be a good paragraph.

What do I do after that? Her mind was a jumble of ideas. *Do I write about the ways people can communicate with angels? I doubt if Ms. Peters will allow that. Maybe I should research the New Age Movement instead. I don't know anything about that, and it might be interesting. I'll take some of these books and then ask Ms. Peters. If I didn't have to write a paper, this research wouldn't be too bad.*

Chapter 4

"Welcome back, Anna," greeted Ms. Peters, "I was sorry to hear about your loss."

"Thank you."

"I see you came prepared to do research. I really didn't expect that, but I am glad you did. Let me know if you need any help," offered Ms. Peters.

"I do have some questions about my topic."

"Okay, let me get the class started and then I'll help you."

Ms. Peters got the class started on their research and said that the outline for the paper did not need to be detailed. "Just a basic framework of the areas you plan to discuss in your paper is all I need. Believe me; this will help you if you know what specific questions you are trying to answer in your research."

Anna had written down both topics, New Age Movement and angels, and had listed questions to be answered about each. She was ready when Ms. Peters called her over to the work table.

"I have two possible topics, and I can't decide which to research," said Anna.

"What was your first choice?" asked Ms. Peters.

"Angels."

"And your second choice?"

"New Age," Anna responded.

"You certainly have selected two interesting topics," Ms. Peters said with a broad smile. "How can I help?"

"If I research angels, I would want to discuss how people communicate with them. That means when I do my presentation, I would like to show how to use a pendulum and angel cards. Would I be allowed to do that?" asked Anna.

"Yes, if it is a part of your research. Over the years I've had students present a wide range of topics. I admit a few did get the principal a little excited, but the projects are supposed to make people think. I don't have any concerns about what you plan to do."

Anna was relieved to hear this.

"What is your interest in the New Age Movement?" asked Ms. Peters with a curious look.

"I've noticed a lot of the books I've been reading have been labeled New Age. I don't understand what New Age and angels have to do with each other, but apparently they go together. I thought if I understood what the New Age Movement is I'd see the connection. Is the movement over or still going on?"

Ms. Peters chuckled and shook her head. "I can't answer that, but I know it began in the late 1960s or early 1970s when many young people opposed the Vietnam War. The anti-establishment movement brought everything into question. Government policies and organized religion were all being scrutinized. Young people were looking for new ideas and an interest in Eastern religions and practices, such as yoga and meditation, grew. You know there is a yoga group here at school, don't you? I think it meets on Wednesdays, or maybe Thursday ... I could go check."

"The New Age Movement?" Anna questioned. She wanted Ms. Peters to stay with her and not go off to another topic like she frequently did.

Ms. Peters got her thoughts back on track and then continued. "I think the New Age Movement was a result of the unrest young people felt. This was a little before my time, but the idea to question government policies and explore new religions still continues."

"What do you think New Age has to do with angels?"

"Maybe your research will tell you. When I think of New Age, I think of the basic beliefs of the eastern religions: reincarnation, meditation, and yoga. This would be a big topic to handle."

"I don't know which to do. What do you think?" asked Anna.

"Oh, no, I can't make that decision; it's your research. Just ask yourself which one you would most enjoy reading about and teaching the class."

"I think I'll stick with angels. I think the New Age Movement is too big of a topic for me. Besides, I want to learn how to communicate with angels. I think it'll be fun showing people how to use the angel cards. I just hope people will be interested," Anna said feeling unsure.

"I think you'll find lots of interest. I know I'll be looking forward to reading your paper and hearing your presentation," said Ms. Peters as another student approached her for help.

Anna's outline was quickly finished. She was eager to read more about communicating with angels. She had listed several ways, but now she needed to learn more about them. The pendulum was one of the oldest divination tools. Anna had heard about them being used to determine the sex of an unborn baby. Her mother or grandmother had said people at baby showers used to dangle the expectant mother's wedding band over her stomach and watch it move in order to determine the sex of the baby. Depending on which way it swung, the sex of the child was revealed. As far as communicating with angels, after a question was asked, a swinging pendulum could answer the questions with yes, no, or uncertain. It all depended on the direction it swung.

The bell rang while Anna was reading about crystals, religious medals, and rings.

Each could be tied to a string and used as a pendulum. She turned in her outline and hurriedly gathered her things. She had two weeks to get this paper finished, and Anna had lots to read and learn. One thing she felt good about was that no one else would be researching angels. Her topic was definitely unique!

The week passed quickly, and Anna read much more than she could ever write about. It was fascinating. In addition to reading books, she continued to read her grandmother's journals. She was drawn to them.

September 16

I want to remember as many stories as I can from the workshop. There are so many, but my favorite has to be the one about "Amazing Grace." Lynn and her husband knew that his cancer was terminal, so they decided that after he passed, he would try to send the hymn "Amazing Grace" to her as a sign that he was near. A friend assured them that this could be done. Lynn said that she has received the song several times over the years, and she is thankful that God has provided this bridge for her and her husband.

Lynn gladly shared with us one incident that she said occurred when she was in desperate need of hearing the lovely hymn. It was the day Hal's ashes were to be spread. Lynn said she waited almost six months before she could bring herself to spread his ashes, and when the day arrived, she still wasn't ready. She was to drive to their favorite spot along the shore and scatter his ashes. Friends and family members were going to meet her there, so she knew she had support. It wasn't enough.

It was a Friday and she had to go to school. She was an elementary teacher. She prayed before leaving home and hoped to hear "Amazing Grace" on the radio. It didn't happen. When she got to school, she was angry. "Why is it on the day I really need to hear from you, I don't?" she asked Hal. She went to her classroom and gathered papers that needed to go to the office. When she passed the music room, she heard the music teacher strumming her guitar and singing. As she listened, tears streamed down her face. "I am so sorry I doubted," she said as the words of "Amazing Grace" surrounded her in the hall. "Please forgive me." It took a few minutes before she could pull herself together. Her prayer had been answered, and her husband let her know he would be with her on this difficult day.

Anna felt the tears roll down her face, and her nose began to drip. Her body was filled with a feeling of perfect peacefulness. She continued to read well into the early morning hours. It was hard to get up for work on Saturday, and when she arrived at her mother's flower shop, she was a half an hour late.

"You're finally here. I have so much to tell you," Karen said as Anna was hanging up her coat. "I've decided to use the money Grandma left me to expand the shop. There is enough land for a small addition, and that is really all I need. The focal point of the new addition will be the angel fountain. I haven't found what I want yet, but I will. I will have an assortment of house plants, a book corner, and hot tea for people to enjoy while they sit by the fountain. I'm not sure what people will sit on, but that will come."

"I like rocking chairs!" Anna said excitedly. "Customers could rock as they look through books and sip tea. It will be a beautiful, tranquil setting."

"A few rocking chairs might work. Relaxation and rocking chairs go together I think. That's a great idea. I want the whole project finished by Valentine's Day. It will be tight, but I think it can be done," said Karen. "Grandma will need to be working from her side to get all this finished by then."

"Do you really think Grandma knows what you are planning and can actually help?"

"Yes. She can see and do things we can't. After all, she can really talk to angels now!" Karen laughed. "I talked to a contractor yesterday, and he said he could begin drawing up plans this week, so I'm ready to expand."

"This will be awesome, Mom," Anna said as she hugged her mother. "Grandma would love this."

"I know. She is my inspiration," Karen said softly. "Come on, we have a lot of work to get done. Susan looks like she needs your help up front. I know you need to leave early today to meet your dad, so you need to hustle."

Chapter 5

Dave Adams was over six feet tall and a handsome man. He had dark, curly hair and blue eyes. When he smiled, a deep dimple on his right cheek appeared. Anna was tall like her father and had inherited his dimple. She wished she had his hair. Hers was a light brown and totally straight, like her mother's. However, she did like her cute new haircut. She hoped the new cut would keep Lauren from giving her a pitiful look and offering to take her to Lauren's stylist.

Anna loved her dad, but his marriage to Lauren had certainly changed her relationship with him. The addition of a stepbrother hadn't helped the situation either. She couldn't help but resent the time her dad spent watching Mark play various sports. He was a son and she was a daughter. The difference was clear. Men always want sons, and now her dad finally had one.

Anna was ready when her dad arrived, and she was starving.

"I thought we'd take you to see the house we found before we go to dinner. It's under construction in the Riverview area. It's close to the high school, and we can be in it by Christmas. Won't that be great?"

"Yes, Dad, that'll be great," said Anna not too convincingly. "Where are we eating? Lorenzo's? I have been looking forward to chicken marsala all day," said Anna.

"Lauren isn't in the mood for Italian, so I thought we'd go to the steak house. I know you love steak, so I didn't think you'd mind. Besides, it's close to the house."

Anna looked at her dad and thought, *It will never change. Lauren will always come first.* Lorenzo's was Anna's favorite restaurant, and it was tradition for her Dad to take her there when he came to town. Anna knew better than to challenge Lauren's choice, so she said, "That'll be fine, Dad. Maybe we can go to Lorenzo's next time." Anna tried to keep the disappointment out of her voice.

"Sure, we can. When we move here, there will be lots of opportunities for us to eat at Lorenzo's. I can hardly wait for you to see the house," Anna's father said as they both got into the car.

Lauren and Mark both seemed pleased with the new house and were glad they found something so quickly.

"Of course, there weren't many houses to choose from that met our specifications," Lauren said in an uppity manner when Anna commented on how quickly they found one. "We are lucky we can still make a few adjustments before the house is finished, and of course we can select all the inside features. It would be awful to move in and then have to change everything the way we did in our Cincinnati house," complained Lauren.

"Not to mention the additional expense," said Anna's dad.

"I wanted our home to be perfect for you," whined Lauren. "I do hope you'll get over what it cost now that we're selling it!"

"Oh, I'm over it. I'm just hoping we will be able to recover the costs of all those improvements when we do sell it," said Dave. He looked lovingly at his wife and added, "You did a great job on the house, honey, and I know this house will be even more beautiful."

"Thanks." Lauren pouted. "As hard as you work, you deserve a house you are proud of."

Oh, please! thought Anna. *I might be sick!* She was relieved when Mark spoke.

"The house is pretty cool. There are lots of trees and a stream runs through the back of the lot, and the walkout basement is awesome. I am glad Mom found a house quickly, so I don't have to come again. I want to stay in Cincinnati as long as possible," said Mark relieved. He had tried all day to be positive about this move. He knew Sweet Grove had a good football team so that was a plus. He also knew that when he moved, Katie would quickly find another boyfriend. He had been dating her for six months and knew she wasn't going to waste time on a long-distance relationship. To be honest, he was beginning to get tired of her self-absorbed ways. Her favorite word was "I": "I want, I think, I need, I, I, I ..."

Mark's thoughts were interrupted when Anna said, "It must be hard to move in the middle of your junior year. I know I would really hate it."

"It sucks, but I don't have a choice. Mom wouldn't stay in Cincy without your dad, so I have to go where she goes, and that is Sweet Grove. I have to make the best of it. At least I can finish football season before we move, which is what really counts. Besides, I know you, and you can introduce me around," Mark said with his engaging smile.

Anna knew the girls would fall all over Mark. He was tall with thick, blond hair, and he had inherited his mother's blue-green eyes. "I will be glad to. Thom Deal lives two doors away, and he's on the football team. He's smart too. I've known him since sixth grade, and he is one of the nicest guys I know."

"Sounds like someone has a crush back there," said Lauren in a childish voice. "Does this Thom have a girlfriend? Maybe Mark will be able to help you out if he and Thom become friends."

"Mom!" said Mark.

"Lauren!" shouted Anna in unison with Mark. "Thom is a good friend, and he happens to like my best friend," said Anna who was thoroughly irritated with Lauren.

"Oh, don't be so sensitive, you two. I was just thinking of the advantages of having a brother or a sister in the same grade. It could come in real handy if someone needs a date. You'll see," Lauren said as they turned onto what would become their new street.

The house was beautiful, but the lot was even more beautiful. Large trees shaded the stone front of the house. A screened porch was on the driveway side of the house. The lot was big enough to handle the five-bedroom home and ensure that neighbors were not too close.

Anna and Mark headed down to the stream after touring the house. Next to the stream was a large weeping willow tree.

"Wow! This is really something. It would be awesome to build a fire down here and roast marshmallows. Maybe this spring we could do that," said Anna eagerly. "This yard is big enough to handle a lot of people. We could invite the entire junior class!"

"That would be cool. We could build a fire pit over here and put volleyball net over there, and there's still room to play football," Mark said planning ahead. "Hey, I'm starving; have you seen enough? I'll go back through the house again if you want, but let's make it fast," Mark said, trying to be considerate.

"I'm good. I need to eat before my stomach starts shouting at me for neglecting it. We were so busy today; I didn't have time to eat lunch," Anna said as they walked back to the house.

"You work for your mom, right?"

"Yeah, I didn't work while my grandmother lived with us, but now that she's gone," Anna's voice broke and she had to pause. "I started back today."

"I'm sorry." Mark wanted to say something comforting but didn't know what else to say.

"Thanks. Let's see if we can get Lauren and Dad out of here!" Anna said quickly in order to change the subject.

It was a quick drive to Pete's Steaks and Potatoes, and fortunately, they didn't have to wait long for a table. Everyone was in a celebratory mood as they ordered their meals, and Anna began to relax. Mark and Anna's dad talked about Ohio State's offensive line and Anna pretended to be interested. She couldn't help but be a little jealous of Lauren's beautiful skin as she looked at her across the table. It was absolutely flawless. Her skin had never seen a freckle that was for sure. Lauren's makeup always looked like it had been done by a professional. Her sea-green eyes and full lips were accentuated perfectly. Like Anna's dad, Lauren had curly hair and her mass of brown ringlets had golden highlights. The highlights were created by her hairdresser and were skillfully applied.

Anna had to admit that Lauren was attractive. She was shorter than Anna and had a stocky build. Her clothes, shoes, and purses were expensive, and she certainly knew how to put it all together. It was hard to miss her bright red finger nails. Anna chuckled to herself thinking how similar Lauren was to the wicked witch in *Snow White*.

Dinner was delicious. Anna's steak was pink in the center the way she liked it, and the stuffed potato was huge. She was tempted to order the chocolate explosion for dessert but decided against it. Their dinner was coming to an end when Anna's father asked about school. Anna gave her usual "everything is fine" response, but that did not end the discussion.

"You mentioned you were working on a research paper. What is your research on?" asked Anna's father.

"Angels."

"Angels? You've got to be kidding!" Anna's dad tended to have a short fuse, and it was showing.

"Yes, Dad, angels," said Anna patiently.

"What class is this?" asked Lauren. "It doesn't sound like very serious research."

"It's for my English class, and it is serious research. You'd be amazed how much has been written about angels," explained Anna.

"What is there to learn? They are white, have wings, and everyone has one. This sounds like a pretty short report," laughed Lauren. "I hope Mark doesn't get this teacher. He is used to challenging teachers and a challenging curriculum."

"Ms. Peters is very challenging. She let us choose our own topics because she wanted us to expand our thinking and discover new things. I have done lots of reading and have learned a lot so far," answered Anna defensively while she dug her fingernails into her napkin.

"Anna's mother and grandmother were very interested in angels," explained Anna's father dryly. "Is that where this came from?" he said, looking at Anna disapprovingly.

"This came from me!" Anna threw her napkin on the table, and her voice began to rise. "I think if more people believed in angels, like Lauren apparently does, they would be happier. They could talk to them and ask for their help. God didn't send us here alone. He provided each of us with guardian angels." Anna's face had turned red and she was trying not to cry, which she usually did when she was really upset.

"It sounds like a topic more suitable for church than school," said Lauren.

"I agree with Lauren," said Anna's dad.

Of course you do! You agree with Lauren about everything, thought Anna angrily. "Well, my teacher approved the topic, and it is due in one week. If anyone is interested, you can read it then," responded Anna heatedly. "I am really tired. Can we go now?"

Anna was silent on the drive home. Lauren talked about her plans for the house and Anna's father was enjoying Lauren's excitement. He didn't seem to remember that Anna was the one he hadn't seen in a couple months. When they reached Anna's house, Dan's car was in the driveway. She was glad she could just go to her room and not have to talk about her evening. Anna quickly said her good-byes and entered her house. After shouting a hello to her mother and Dan, she went into her grandmother's room.

Anna's grandmother's favorite sweater was in the closet. It was large and soft. The dark-blue color was faded and the elbows were worn thin, but Grandma's smell still clung to the fabric. Anna lovingly wrapped herself up in thoughts of Grandma, and she gently rocked in Grandma's chair. Her eyes rested on Grandma's angel cards.

Anna had never seen her grandmother use the cards. In fact, Grandma had kept them out of sight. Anna's mother had found them for Anna to use in her report. There was a booklet with the cards, and Anna began to read the instructions: pray, ask the question, lay down three to five cards, read, and think about the message. *Sounds pretty easy*, Anna thought.

"What advice can you give me?" she asked her angels aloud. She shuffled the cards until she was ready and laid down three cards: Align Your Thoughts, Confidence in God, Romance Is Near. Each card had an explanation and there was further information in the booklet. Anna was immediately excited by the romance card. She and Ross had broken up six months ago and now he was dating Josie. It hurt to see them together, but he had been a real jerk. She wasn't ready to go as far as he wanted. If she wasn't ready to play in the big league, he told her, then he couldn't take the sexual frustration. She wondered if Josie was ready for the big league or not.

Anna assumed she was to read from left to right, so she began with Romance Is Near: *Your angels know your desire for romance. Heal all past and current relationships that may be dragging you down by sending them love. Prayers of love are great healers. Romance is on the horizon.* "Wow! This is so cool. I do need to get over Ross. Grandma told me I needed to close the window so a new guy can walk in the front door. That's what my angels are saying too."

The next card was Align Your Thoughts: *Carefully monitor your thoughts. If you desire happiness, think positively. Forgive quickly, look for loving solutions, and show gratitude for all blessings daily. Sunshine creates warmth.* "I certainly have heard this before. Both Mom and Grandma talked about keeping my thoughts on what I want and not giving any time to things I don't want," Anna said.

Anna looked at the last card. Have Confidence in God: *You are never alone. God works with you and through you if you ask. Angels are always available to guide and support you.* "I prayed right before Grandma died, and she still died," Anna said. "A lot of good that did."

"But it did, sweetheart."

Anna looked up, wondering. "Grandma?"

"It was my time."

"Grandma?" Anna could not see her grandmother, but the room smelled like her grandmother's favorite perfume. She clearly heard her grandmother's voice. Tears began filling Anna's eyes. "Oh, Grandma, I miss you so much. Why did you have to leave me?" There was no answer, but Anna knew Grandma would have told her that she would always be close by.

Pulling back the covers of her Grandmother's bed, Anna crawled in, still wrapped in the old blue sweater. "Maybe Grandma will come to me again in my dreams," Anna said as she quietly cried herself to sleep.

Chapter 6

Anna wasn't sure how to tell her mom about Grandma's visit, so she decided to just come right out and say it. "Mom, Grandma was here last night."

Karen slowly put her coffee cup down and said, "Tell me about it."

"I was in her room using her angel cards, and I got a card that said God and his angels were always with me. I was angry that they took Grandma away even though I'd been praying for her. She told me it was her time."

"You know it was, honey. I think God and his angels helped us get through her sickness and her death. I know I couldn't have made it through everything without it."

"I guess you're right. I just miss her so much." Anna's voice was quivering, and she was trying not to cry.

Karen hugged Anna tightly and said, "I'm glad Mom didn't have to endure anymore pain. I'm also glad she spoke to you." Karen hesitated and then said, "And a little envious."

"It was like you said about that workshop; it wasn't scary at all. It was her. She was with me. It was wonderful. She really is close by and not gone forever," Anna said trying to reassure herself.

"You are right about that," Karen said as she released Anna from their hug. "We need to hurry if we want to make it to church."

"What if we don't want to make it?"

"Well, I guess we just enjoy a nice morning together before I have to leave for work."

"I vote for that option."

"Okay with me. I could use a quiet morning with my favorite daughter."

"You and Dad both use that corny line. Of course I'm your favorite daughter; I'm your *only* daughter!" Anna said while shaking her head. *My parents may be divorced, but they say the same dumb things*, she thought.

"How was last night?"

"Dinner was good, and Lauren was her usual charming self. She really is hard to like, Mom."

"I know, but you love your Dad, so you have to be nice and try to find the good in her. What about Mark? How's he handling the move?" asked Karen.

"Better than I would. He gets to stay in Cincinnati until football season is over, so that makes him happy. Once he gets here, the girls will fall all over him. He is almost in the gorgeous category. He and I get along, so no problem there. Lauren did something right; she had a nice son."

Karen poured herself another cup of coffee and got out the pie from last night. "How about apple pie for breakfast?"

"I'd love it! Grandpa always liked pie for breakfast, didn't he?"

"Yes. He claimed that as kids they would frequently have pie for breakfast. He said his mother would make breakfast pies. I think they were probably filled with eggs and meat like quiches, but he always talked about fruit pies. I don't know, maybe they had both."

Anna and her mother ate in comfortable silence. Each had wonderful memories of both grandparents to review in their minds.

Anna interrupted the silence by saying, "You never told me what finally made Grandpa a believer in angels."

"It was the hummingbird," said Karen.

"The hummingbird?" asked Anna intrigued.

"Dad thought the reason we found pennies was because we were looking for them. All the unusual places we found them didn't convince him that our angels were leaving them. So your grandmother suggested he give it a try for himself by asking his angels to send him something as a sign. He had been waiting for a hummingbird to show up in his garden for a couple weeks after hearing from others that the hummingbirds had returned to their yards. He decided to ask his angels to send him a hummingbird as a sign. He sat in the yard and prayed and waited. He must have thought that if he sat long enough one would appear. It doesn't work that way. The sign usually appears when you least expect it."

"Why is that?"

"I'm not really sure. Mary Matson would probably say that the anxiety of waiting creates negative energy and it interferes with the person's ability to receive. Me? I don't know; I'm just glad to receive a sign.

"Well, Grandpa decided the test was over so he went inside. The next morning he went outside with his coffee and paper to begin his morning, which was his summer routine, and began reading. The wind blew some of the paper on the patio floor, and when he bent to pick it up, he saw the hummingbird. It was at one of the big flowerpots. He just sat and watched. He said it took a while for it all to sink in, but it did. That was the beginning for him. Before he died, he had several stories he liked to tell about his hummingbirds."

"Tell me one," said Anna softly.

"Okay, let me think. I've got it. He called it his January hummingbird. Dad hated January. He hated the cold, he hated the short gray days, and he hated that he couldn't even take a walk in the neighborhood because there was too much ice and snow on the sidewalks.

"He sat in his chair and muttered about all the things he hated. Mom told him he needed to change his attitude because he was bringing her down. He grumbled, 'I'll change my attitude when something good happens to make me change it.' He continued to sit in his chair and began going through a pile of magazines. He was on about his fourth magazine when he turned to a picture and an article about hummingbirds. He called Grandma to come quickly.

'When she entered the room, he turned the magazine around so she could see the picture of a hummingbird. He cut the picture out of the magazine and kept it as a reminder that his angels were always around to help and support him. Dad always said that was the nicest kick in the pants he had ever received. After that, he did improve his attitude and said he was grateful to his angels for giving him exactly what he needed. He always carried the picture in his wallet," Karen said.

"That's why he bought those crystal hummingbirds, isn't it?" asked Anna.

"Yes, he wanted to be able to see a hummingbird every day. And that's why Grandma had them hanging in the window in her room here. It was a daily reminder of Dad and of God's love. They brought her a lot of comfort," Karen said as she looked at Anna.

"That's a nice story. I have read and heard so many stories in the past two weeks. I can't believe I didn't know this before. Just think, if I hadn't been assigned this research project, I still wouldn't know all these family stories."

"How are you doing on your angel report?"

"Good. My paper is due Friday, and I present the following week. I'll find out tomorrow what day. I need to practice my presentation because we are going to be timed. I have five minutes. I have so much information; I don't know how to give just five minutes worth," Anna said worriedly.

"I'm sure you'll figure it out. I'll be glad to be your test audience when you're ready. Now, I really need to get ready for work," said Karen as she stood and rinsed out her coffee mug at the sink. "What are your plans for today?"

"Maddie and I are going to do something later. I might as well get my paper finished since I'm in the mood. Tonight is spaghetti night, right?"

"Right, but I thought I'd let Lorenzo do the cooking instead of me," said Karen as she tossed Anna's hair.

"Anything from Lorenzo's is fine with me."

Instead of finishing her paper, Anna went upstairs and read more of her grandmother's journals.

November 11

> I can't fully express how empty I feel inside. To say I miss Ed doesn't even begin to cover the extent of my sorrow. I am thankful for my family and friends and my angels.

> As I write this, I am holding the penny that I found in the parking lot of the funeral home after Ed's service. Karen, Anna, and I were about to get into the car, and as I opened the door, I saw a penny on the ground. I knew my angels were showing their support.

December 21

My first Christmas without Ed. The tree is up, and I have been baking up a storm with my sweet Anna. Tomorrow I help at the church's food pantry. This is a busy time, but a part of me is missing. I feel blessed that I hear one of my favorite Christmas carols every time I turn on the radio. It's almost automatic. It doesn't matter what time of day it is either. If I'm listening, I hear "Hark the Herald Angels." I don't think it is a coincidence. I think my angels are telling me they are with me. Merry Christmas, my sweet angel friends!

Chapter 7

Anna was assigned to present on Monday, the first day of presentation week. She was both excited and nervous. She had practiced twice, once with Maddie and once with her Mom; she knew she could meet her time limit. Anna hoped the class wouldn't think angels were a dumb topic. She had been so sure that being unique and totally different from what everyone else was doing was the way to go, but now as she was about to present, she was scared she'd be laughed at.

As required, Anna began with a short history of angels. She taught the class that people in various religions believe in angels. She wanted her classmates to know that believing in angels was not some fad. Most of the kids gave Anna their polite attention. However, when she came to the part of her presentation about how to communicate with angels, her audience became genuinely interested. All eyes were on Anna, and many were leaning forward so they would be sure not to miss anything she was demonstrating.

She showed the class how to ask a question and receive an answer with a deck of angel cards. She also showed the class a pendulum. Someone shouted, "No way," as the pendulum began to swing. Others argued over whether Anna was causing it to move. Every presenter was allowed to take a few questions at the end of his or her presentation, and Anna saw many hands in the air when she was told her five minutes were up.

"I thought your presentation was pretty interesting, but I don't believe we each have an angel just waiting to talk to us. If that's true, why hasn't mine knocked me on the head a few times or shouted in my ear?" asked Jeff as he leaned back in his chair.

"You have to be willing to hear them. If you don't believe then how could you see or hear? I think it's like having a closed door. You have to open it to see who's there."

"Can you use those cards to ask questions about someone besides yourself?" Tara asked from the front row. She had listened intently throughout the entire presentation.

"Sure. There are a lot of people who do angel readings. Many call themselves intuitivists, because they have developed their intuitive powers to be able to not only read the cards but to sense a deeper meaning for their clients."

"Could you do that?" continued Tara.

"I don't know. I haven't tried. I know I'd be nervous to try to read for someone else," Anna said, and then she called upon another student. "Amber."

"How are those cards different from Tarot cards? And isn't fortune telling a practice of witchcraft?" stated Amber with a smug look on her face. She was editor for the school newspaper and always felt the need to ask questions as if she was an investigative reporter.

"I don't know anything about witchcraft or Tarot cards. I do know that the angel cards are filled with loving, supportive comments. Readers usually pray before they use the cards, so that doesn't sound like witchcraft. I don't think there are any witches outside of fairy tales. There are Wiccans, and their religion is called Wicca. I read a book about angels written by a Wiccan, so obviously some Wiccans must believe in angels," Anna explained patiently.

"Anna can take one more question, and then it's time for Aaron to present," said Ms. Peters trying to keep the class on time.

Becca Stitch seldom asked questions in class. She seemed to either isolate herself or the class avoided her. Whatever it was, she was one of the easily overlooked persons in the class. "I've used a Ouija board before. I ask questions, and I get answers. Isn't that like your angel cards?" she asked.

"I've used a Ouija board before too. I don't know how the Ouija moved, but we did get answers. I believe that since I pray and ask for my angels to be with me, I know where the answers are coming from. I know I am asking my angels for an answer, and I don't know who I was asking when I used the Ouija board."

Becca looked at Anna and smiled shyly; Anna returned the smile. They had made a connection, and they both felt it.

"Time's up. Aaron, we are ready for you." Ms. Peters effectively ended the questioning, but there were many questions Anna's classmates had not been given time to ask.

"Hey, I heard you were quite a hit this morning," said Maddie at lunch.

"Where did you hear that?" wondered Anna as she reached for her sandwich.

"Tara Sanders is in my history class, and she was talking about you. She said you told her you'd read the angel cards for her," reported Maddie as she carefully watched Anna's face for her reaction.

"Yeah, she talked me into trying. I just don't want to disappoint her," said Anna uncertainly. She was already regretting saying she'd try.

"Well, you'd better be good at it because she was telling everyone about it. She acts like you are the new Sylvia Browne or something. Girls will probably stand in line to have the 'All-Powerful Anna' read for them," Maddie said. Her disapproval was evident as she spoke.

That was not what Anna wanted to hear. She didn't want to be the next Sylvia Browne. She had just wanted to show her classmates what she had learned, and of course get a good grade. An A would be nice. Her research really had been for her. It had helped her feel closer to her grandmother.

Maddie's comment turned out to be quite prophetic. Anna couldn't believe the number of people who stopped her in the hall and asked her if she would do an angel reading for them. People were calling her "Angel Girl." Anna wasn't prepared for all the attention she was receiving. If she could take back telling Tara she'd read for her, she would. She hated being the topic of the day!

Tara came to her house after dinner that night. Anna said a prayer and asked for guidance for Tara. She shuffled the cards thoroughly and laid down five cards. She read what was written on the cards and waited for Tara to respond. Tara was quick to know what three of the cards were referring to. Anna used the booklet that came with the cards and read a more complete description of what the other two cards could be referring to. After hearing the possible meanings, Tara knew immediately what her angels were telling her. Anna felt relieved that the reading had gone well. She realized that Tara was the one who had understood the message. All she had done was ask the questions for her and read what was written on the cards and in the booklet. *This isn't difficult at all*, she thought.

Because of her success with Tara, Anna agreed to read for other girls. The problem was the more people she read, the more others wanted a reading too. A month after her presentation, she was doing about five readings a week and didn't know how to stop.

"When your grandmother and I went to the angel workshop, we were told not to do any readings for free. I thought Mary was wrong; now I know Mary was right. If you continue to use your talent freely, people will take advantage of you. You really need to charge a fee," said Karen thoughtfully. "People won't be asking as frequently if they have to pay for it."

"I can't ask my friends to pay me. Mom, I just couldn't do that," Anna looked at her mom willing her to understand.

"You are using your time, which is in short supply. How much time do you spend with each girl?"

"About a half an hour for each reading."

"I know you are helping your friends and it is fun, but you need to set limits and maybe charging a small fee will help the girls respect your time."

"I could ask to be paid in cookies but not money," Anna said with an impish grin.

"Cute," Karen said smiling. "With Christmas coming, I'll need you more at the store, so you won't be available to do many readings. But I still want you to think of something the girls can do for you, so I don't think you are being taken advantage of."

"I could ask for a donation to the food pantry with each reading. That way I would be getting paid but not feel guilty about taking money from my friends. How does that sound?"

"I think that is a wonderful idea. I will put a jar on the counter in the store for donations to the food pantry too. There was an article in the paper saying how low the supplies are this year. That's a perfect solution," Karen said as she handed Anna a plate.

It was nice to be able to sit down and talk. Anna had always felt close to her mom, but learning about angels had brought them closer.

"Mom, it's weird how the cards can pinpoint something that is going on in a person's life," Anna said as she moved her broccoli away from her chicken. She believed each food deserved its own space. "I don't know personal things about these girls who I read the cards for. I just pray and ask for information and then lay down the cards. I do what you said. I read the cards and explain what they could indicate, and the person takes it from there. They are the ones explaining what the card means, not me. They could really do it for themselves," said Anna.

"Yes, they could. They need to believe they can get answers to their questions on their own and not rely on someone else. Maybe I should sell angel reading cards in my shop. What do you think?" asked Karen.

"I think it's a great idea. That will take some pressure off me. The sooner you can get them the better!" said Anna. She liked the idea of having friends she could talk to about angels and other mystical things. She was beginning to feel different, but she couldn't put it into words. Maybe more peaceful? She needed other girls who were excited about learning how to develop their sixth sense like she was. This whole field of metaphysics was new to her, and it helped to have others to talk to about it.

Maddie had thought Anna's angel research topic was cool at first. After Anna began doing readings and became the talk of the school, Maddie's attitude completely changed. She teased Anna about how she needed to watch herself now that her best friend talked to angels. She said she didn't want to rack up negative points with the heavenly realm. Maddie tried to be light-hearted about what she said, but the undertone was clear. Anna made her feel uncomfortable.

Anna was glad to be working at her mother's flower shop again. She liked the variety of plants and colors that each season brought to the store.

"We should use the angel theme throughout the shop, Mom. Angels aren't just for Christmas. People buy and use angel items all year long. I love the valentines with the chubby, little cupids shooting arrows. It's funny; now I notice angel items everywhere. One of my teachers even has a coffee mug with angels on it."

"I've been thinking the same thing about selling more angel items. Since we will have a beautiful angel fountain, we might as well have angels everywhere. I ordered several new angels and they arrived yesterday. I saved them for you to unpack. I bought little angel cards to attach to all the holiday plants that will be delivered, and I ordered a new line of angel figurines. The shop will literally be filled with angels by Christmas." Karen laughed.

Dinner was filled with plans, laughter, and a wonderful feeling of closeness. Both women hoped the angel addition would bring new business into the shop. Karen was only too aware of the businesses in the area that had been forced to close. New ideas were essential, she thought, to keep her customers coming. This might be just what was needed in a sluggish economy.

Anna was excited about Christmas and the changes coming to her Mom's flower shop, but Christmas also meant that Anna's father and family would be moving to Sweet Grove; she was anxious about how that was going to work. She talked to her father every week and had seen him once since the steak house dinner. He had asked how her presentation went, but he didn't know she was doing readings for people as a result of her presentation. Anna knew that he wouldn't approve. What was she going to do with a stepbrother at her school? He would certainly hear about the readings and then her dad would know. She hoped that all this would be forgotten by the time Mark arrived.

Chapter 8

"**A**nna, did you buy a school newspaper yet?" asked Maddie between classes.

"No, I'm going to at lunch. Why?"

"There is an article about you in it. Be prepared," warned Maddie with a slight look of satisfaction on her face. "See ya at lunch," she said as she folded her paper and walked away.

"So, are you an angel or a witch?" teased Thom Deal when Anna sat next to him in history class. He handed her the school paper, which was turned to the editorial page in response to her puzzled expression.

The Crucible was an outstanding production and all who contributed should be congratulated. The question is this. Do we have our own Tituba right here at Sweet Grove High? Fortune-telling led to a lot of trouble in Salem. Can history repeat itself here? Over the past few weeks, the female population of Sweet Grove has been frantically having their fortunes told by the Angel Girl. Many of these ladies have the misconception that this person has a special gift of knowing things and seeing things. They have begun wearing angel pins, and they talk about the Angel Girl like she is a saint. Fellow students, wise up! Sweet Grove doesn't need an angel cult any more than Salem needed a coven of witches. Wake up and smell the brew in this angel's cauldron!

Anna felt sick to her stomach as she handed the paper back to Thom. Why would Amber write such a hateful article about her? People around her were watching to see her reaction to the editorial. She calmly put her history book on her desk and stared at the cover. Anna's mind was spinning as she tried to replay all that had happened since her presentation. Anna had noticed girls wearing angel pins, but she hadn't given it much thought. Now that she thought about it, kids were watching what they said around her. Nan, a girl Anna had known since elementary school, had apologized for saying, "Oh, shit!" in her presence. Anna also remembered that a group of girls had stopped talking about another girl when she walked up. *Do kids think I am like an angel priestess or something?* She wondered. Her thoughts were interrupted when Mr. Coates personally told her to open her book to page 459.

Class was a blur. Anna had no idea what had been discussed. She wanted to find a place to hide. As soon as the bell rang, Thom said, "I'm walking you to your next class. You don't look so good."

"Thanks, Thom. I feel like I just came down with the flu. You've known me forever. Have I changed somehow? Do kids really think I lead an angel cult or something?"

"If you do, I'll join. I like the idea of being in an all-girls cult that believes in angels. I bet they would treat me heavenly!" laughed Thom.

Anna punched Thom in the arm and gave him a weak laugh. "Be careful, I just might use my powers on you."

"As long as you don't turn me into a frog, I'm on your side. It might be time to have a guy have one of your angel readings. How about it?" asked Thom.

"I think I've read my last cards for a while. But thanks for being so nice. You really are a good friend."

They arrived at Anna's class, and Thom needed to get to his. "If you change your mind, I'm willing. Hang in there. See ya later."

Anna couldn't help but feel better. Thom is really nice and cute, but he's always liked Maddie. *Don't read anything in this,* she told herself. All eyes were on Anna as she took her seat in class. She tried to calm herself by thinking, *You haven't done anything wrong. All this will pass in a few days.* Five minutes into class, Anna was called to the vice principal's office.

"Anna, I thought it would be better if I talked to you instead of Principal Bates. You seem to have created a bit of a situation," Ms. Carson said.

Ann sat and waited. Ms. Carson was dressed in her usual dark suit. She was always very uptight, and most kids avoided her if possible. She was the rule enforcer and everyone knew it. Anna actually wished that she had been summoned by Principal Bates. He could be cool at times.

"Do you have anything to say about the newspaper article?" asked Ms. Carson as she leaned forward in her chair.

"Have I done something wrong?" asked Anna timidly.

"That is what I am trying to find out. I need to be sure that no unauthorized groups have been organized in our school." Ms. Carson straightened herself and folded her hands on her desk as she continued. "I know what you have been doing, and I am very concerned. The girls I have talked to claim that you actually have some mystical power. Is that true?"

"Ms. Carson, I don't possess special powers. I possess a deck of angel cards and a belief that if I pray and ask for guidance, my prayer will be answered. I don't know why Amber would write such awful things about me in the school paper. People like knowing they have angels. That's what I've done, made people aware of their angels. None of the readings I have done have been here at school." Anna hated being in here defending herself. She felt embarrassed and angry at the same time. After all, this all began as a school research project.

"I think it best if you put these readings on hold for a while. I haven't seen anything negative come from this yet, but I must be watchful." Ms. Carson stood as she spoke. "I admit on the surface, girls talking about angels and wearing angel pins seems like a nice thing. But I've learned over the years that what appears nice at first can easily change. I think it would be wise if you could use your influence to stop this angel movement before it gets out of hand. Would you be willing to do that?"

"Ms. Carson, I can't tell people to stop wearing angel pins. In fact, I think I'll start wearing one. You're right when you said this was a nice thing. People are acting nicer lately. If I am not doing readings on school property then I guess there is no reason to stop. Thanks, Ms. Carson, you've made me see the good that has come from this. Can I go back to class now?" Anna stood as she spoke.

"Don't say I didn't warn you when this all blows up! Yes, go back to class. Remember you are here to get an education, not teach about angels," Ms. Carson said.

With that, Anna was ushered out of the office. Ms. Carson forgot to put a time on the hall pass, so Anna went to restroom to collect her thoughts. She entered the last stall and sat down. She took a few deep breaths and tried to feel good about standing up for herself with Ms. Carson. It wasn't like her at all! Anna had always been the "good girl," and now she had actually been called to the office. As she opened the stall's door to leave, she noticed something on the floor next to the sink. It was a penny. "Thanks, angels!" Anna said softly and walked to class feeling much better.

Anna was the hot topic of conversation at lunch. Girls wearing angel pins surrounded her when she entered the cafeteria. All of them were indignant at what had been written in the school paper. They too felt Amber had attacked them. One girl suggested that Amber was just jealous, and another said she was an atheist. Tara said she was glad Anna had shown her how to use the cards, and a few girls excitedly told about asking their angels for signs and receiving them. Anna had not made them believers; their guardian angels had.

Becca Stitch, the shy girl from Anna's English class, said she had asked for a sign and had received a fat robin. She laughed as she explained that she had told her angels that she was new at this, so the sign would have to be something she wouldn't miss. Two days later, as she left her home for school, a fat robin was sitting on her mailbox singing. As she got closer, he stopped singing but tilted his head and continued to sit on the mailbox. She said she was probably two feet away and he began singing again. Becca was certain that the robin was her angelic sign.

It was great that Becca had found other girls who shared her interest in angels. She certainly was not an outsider anymore. Many girls had joined the yoga club the health teacher started, and apparently they were beginning to discuss a variety of metaphysical topics in addition to doing yoga. They asked Anna to join them, but the club met the same night she worked. After the newspaper article, she decided she'd talk to her mom about switching her work schedule to another night. She realized how much she needed the support of these girls.

Maddie was not pleased with Anna and made it clear at lunch. "It took you long enough to shake off your new friends and finally get to our table. Lunch is half over."

"They wanted to be sure I was all right. That was a pretty nasty article Amber wrote," Anna said as she unwrapped her ham sandwich.

"It was a little rough, but she did make a good point about all those girls wearing angel pins. I think they've gotten a little extreme in their angel devotion," Maddie said without looking up at Anna.

"Really?" Anna said in a surprised voice.

"Really," Maddie responded emphatically.

Anna had planned on telling Maddie about Ms. Carson calling her to the office, but she quickly changed her mind. She wasn't sure which side Maddie would be on, hers or Ms. Carson's. She couldn't take any more disapproval, especially from her best friend.

Chapter 9

The holiday dance at Sweet Grove High was more of a giant party than a dance. People dressed in bright holiday colors and wore Santa hats, reindeer antlers, and battery-powered blinking lights. It was always a lot of fun. It was also a tradition that people didn't attend as couples. Therefore, it was usually the biggest social event of the year.

Maddie and Anna arrived and quickly joined a group of girls. Many compliments and squeals were heard as the girls reacted to each other's creativity. Boys did find their girls, and couples did dance, but impromptu skits were always the best part of the evening. The band's break time was show time for many of the drama kids.

The first skit was about how Rudolph couldn't get a date for New Year's Eve. Maddie had been in that skit. A group of girls sang and danced with *Frosty the Snowman*, and a boy and a girl did a funny skit about what Santa was going to bring them. The band was coming back when a group of boys dressed as angels ran out on the floor.

"Good evening, students, I am so glad to be able to be with you tonight. I am Gabe, and these are members of my angel band. Notice, we only play harps." Members of the group twirled and bowed. They fluffed their large, white feathery wings, flapped their arms, and picked at their harp strings. "Some of your fellow students have been advertising for us. We wanted to come and personally thank them. The angel girls are keeping us pretty busy. It gets so boring just hanging around people and not being noticed. Now we actually have people talking to us! The boys pretended to play their harps and sang: "Joy to the world, so many pretty girls.

And let, them all, love us! Let ev-ery heart, pre-pare to love, and girls and angels sing."

"Join in!" shouted Thom as he led the crowd in singing to the tune of *Joy to the World.*

"And girls and angels sing, and girls, and more girls, and angels sing!"

The crowd loved them, and amidst the applause and laughter, Thom shouted, "Come on, girls, show us some love!"

The angel boys were thrilled they had been such a hit and threw down their harps and ran into the audience looking for girls. As far as the boys were concerned, all girls are angels. The girls laughed and willingly gave hugs, and some of the guys received kisses. Anna gladly gave her angel guy, Thom, a big hug and a kiss on the cheek. She loved the skit. It was fun to make light of all the crazy talk that had surrounded her and the other girls.

The evening ended with a slow dance for Thom and Anna. It felt nice to be in Thom's arms. Once again, Anna realized what a great guy Thom was. Those blues eyes could make her heart skip a beat that was for sure. *If only he'd get over Maddie,* Anna thought as she swayed to the music and thought how nice it would be to really kiss him.

The days quickly flew by, and the two week Christmas break was eagerly anticipated. Christmas was a time of mixed emotions for Anna. She missed her grandmother and their holiday traditions. They had made Christmas cookies together every year since she had been old enough to push the rolling pin. Grandma and Anna had taken over decorating the Christmas tree about five years ago because Karen was so busy at the store. They would play Christmas carols, eat cookies, and reminisce over the collection of ornaments.

With Grandma gone, Anna and Karen couldn't find time to bake cookies, but they decorated the tree together along with Dan. It was fun for Anna, having her mother and Dan help with the tree. Dan assembled the tree quickly and efficiently, and Karen carefully wove the white lights from front to back as she surrounded the tree. Placing the lights correctly had been important to Grandma. She would always say the light had to shine from the center of the tree out, just the way light shines from a person. Selecting ornaments and determining their placements was lots of fun. They laughed, sang carols, and ate popcorn. *Perhaps she and her mother were starting a new tradition*, Anna thought, and she didn't mind that Dan was a part of it.

The flower shop stayed open until six in the evening on Christmas Eve. That meant Karen didn't get home until seven. Dan and Anna had dinner waiting when she arrived. Anna had made sugar cookies while she listened to carols in the morning. In the middle of mixing the ingredients, she smelled a familiar scent. It was Grandma's favorite perfume. She breathed in deeply and knew her Grandma was paying her a visit.

"Merry Christmas, Grandma," she said aloud. "I am glad you came to make cookies with me." This was the best Christmas gift Anna could have received.

Christmas evening, Anna went to her dad's house. Since Lauren and Mark were not moving for another month, the house was only half furnished. The dining room and family room had furniture, and her dad had a bed to sleep in, so it was a good beginning.

Lauren had baked a ham and made scalloped potatoes for dinner, and they had decorated a tree. Since Lauren usually decorated two trees in Cincinnati, Dave brought one of the trees to Sweet Grove and decorated it in scarlet and gray for the Ohio State Buckeyes. The tree was covered with buckeyes, red and gray ornaments, and ornaments with the numbers of famous former players. Her dad went a little crazy when it came to the Buckeyes.

Lauren and Mark planned on staying in Sweet Grove until the end of Christmas break, so the conversation turned to Anna. "Anna, how about you bringing some friends over for Mark to meet sometime next week?" asked her dad.

"Okay, when?"

"Next Tuesday or Wednesday would be good," answered Lauren.

"I work on Wednesday, so I guess it has to be Tuesday," replied Anna unenthusiastically. She knew she had to come. Families! Hopefully Maddie and Thom would be able to come with her. She had told Thom about Mark and that he was planning on playing football for Sweet Grove next year. Maddie said she didn't have any special plans for break, so Anna thought she'd be available.

"Thanks for coming with me," Anna said to Maddie and Thom as they arrived at her dad's house the following Tuesday. "Mark is kind of bummed about having to move here, so I promised I'd introduce him to a few people. He really wants to meet you, Thom, so he can find out about the football team."

"Hey, no problem," said Thom.

"I wanted to see your dad's house, so this works for me," Maddie said as she got out of the car. "Wow! This is some house! Lead on, Anna!"

Mark opened the door, and Anna introduced her friends. He gave them a tour of the house, and they settled down in front of the stone fireplace in the family room. Maddie acted like she had lockjaw; Anna had never seen her so quiet. When the girls went to the kitchen to get a couple diet sodas, Anna asked her if something was wrong.

"You didn't tell me how hot Mark is. He is absolutely gorgeous! Don't you realize that?" Maddie stared at her friend in wonder.

"Yeah, I know, but I can't get very excited over my stepbrother. I think Thom is pretty hot. Don't you? He's tall, has beautiful eyes, and he's so sweet." Anna looked at Maddie, wanting to see her reaction.

"Thom is hot for you."

"Yeah, right. He's liked you forever," Anna said.

"I know he has, but I have never gone out with him, have I? He is just too nice for me. Anyway, he doesn't like me anymore. You are so dense. What did you think that angel number was all about at the Christmas dance? And he asked you to dance, not me. He's into you; wake up! Besides, he's really not in Mark's league. Mark is amazing. I swear I just melt listening to him talk. And that smile! I am sooo glad you brought me here tonight."

"Easy, girl. I think you're hyperventilating. So, you really think Thom likes me?"

"Open your eyes, Anna. It's obvious. Jeez!" Maddie said as she flung her long, blonde hair and grabbed a soda.

The girls rejoined the boys who were talking football. Maddie sat on the floor in front of the fire, close to Mark's feet. She was determined to make a memorable impression.

"So you won't be starting school until next semester?" asked Maddie, giving him her "I'm so interested" look.

"No, Dave has to be here, but the house in Cincinnati hasn't sold, so Mom and I can stay there. It also makes it easier to transfer my credits if I wait until the semester end," explained Mark.

"Are you interested in theater? We have a great theater department," Maddie said. Her interest in Mark was so intense; Anna could actually feel it across the room.

"Maddie is one of Sweet Grove's most talented thespians," interjected Thom.

"I don't know about that, but I do like being on stage." Maddie blushed when she spoke.

"She was awesome in *The Crucible*," continued Thom. "Wasn't she, Anna?"

"Yes, awesome. You aren't into the theater are you, Mark?" asked Anna.

"Only as a member of the audience. There wouldn't be theater without an audience you know. I've gone to the *Broadway Series* with Mom in Cincinnati, and I liked most of the shows. My high school has a pretty good drama department, I think," Mark said smiling at Maddie, finally seeming to notice her.

Maddie was positively glowing from being in Mark's presence. She had to concentrate on what she was saying so Mark wouldn't think she was an idiot. "Anna is in the theater program too. We are both trying out for the spring musical. Since you are an experienced audience member, I'm sure you'll be there," Maddie said coyly.

I am going to be sick, thought Anna. *Maddie is simply gushing over Mark.* She looked over at Thom, and he was looking at *her.* Maybe there was something there. Thom had been paying a lot of attention to her lately. She should have caught on when he came to find her after the angel performance. *I really am dense. I just thought he was being the nice guy he always is. Duh! He did all that for me! What an idiot I am*, Anna thought.

"Would anyone like to go bowling tomorrow night? Mark only has a few nights here, so we need to make the most of them. What do you say Angel Girl? Are you up for it?" Thom said as he put his hand on Anna's shoulder.

"Angel Girl? What's that all about?" asked Mark as he turned his attention to Anna.

"Oh, that is just a nickname from the research project I did on angels. Remember? No big deal. Thom just likes to tease me, that's all."

"It is a big deal. After she presented to her English class, the whole school was talking about her. There was even an editorial about her in the school paper. Anna used her cards to do angel readings for a lot of girls, and the girls started wearing angel pins like they were in some club. The editor of the school paper accused her of starting a cult, and she was even called to the principal's office," Maddie told him eagerly. She had been able to tell the whole story in one breath, while Anna was trying to signal her to shut up.

"Readings? You do readings?" asked Lauren. They all turned to see that Dave and Lauren had entered the room.

No, no, no, this can't be happening, thought Anna. Looking at Thom and then to her father, she answered, "Sometimes." She looked down at her hands instead of her dad.

"Why on earth would you do that? Did you get into trouble at school over this angel nonsense?" asked her dad angrily.

"I was called to the vice principal's office, but I didn't get into trouble. And I did a few readings for some girls because they really wanted me too, and I couldn't say no without hurting their feelings," Anna said in a meek voice.

"Can you *really* do readings?" asked Lauren skeptically.

"I helped the girls do their own readings is a better way to put it." Anna looked at Lauren wondering what would come next. She braced herself.

"Could you read me?" Lauren asked pointedly with an arched eyebrow.

Anna was blown away. She never would have anticipated that response from Lauren.

"What? Are you crazy too? You can't encourage her in doing this. I don't approve of her getting into this anymore than I did her mother. I won't have it! This is my house, and I simply won't have it!" Dave said about ready to explode.

"Perhaps we should discuss this at another time. We certainly don't want to ruin the kids' evening by talking about it now," Lauren said smoothly. "I thought we should order some pizza since Mark hasn't eaten in the last two hours. He's probably famished! What kind should I order?"

Dave gave Anna "the look," which meant the topic wasn't finished, and it wasn't. Two evenings later, Dave called Anna. He was not pleased with her interest in angels and wasn't sure how to talk to her about it. When Karen had started reading the New Age books, he hadn't liked it. She started talking about receiving signs and meditating to become more attuned with her higher self. She did all sorts of crazy stuff, and he didn't want Anna going down that same "loony" path.

"Anna, I just want you to listen before you say anything," Dave began. "You know that I love you and want what's best for you. I am concerned that this interest in angels will bring you unhappiness."

"Dad, I—"

"Let me finish. You have been raised in the church the way your mother and I were. Your mother has done a good job of keeping you on track. Of course there are angels because the Bible talks about them. But to believe they actually send people signs, well, I think that is stretching their capabilities. Reasonable people do not think that finding a penny or hearing a song means anything supernatural has occurred. I want you to think rationally about this. I also want to protect you from criticism. Teenagers can be cruel, and I hate it if you became a target of ridicule."

"Can I talk now?" Anna asked hesitantly.

"Yes."

"I read several books by different authors when I did my research. I have experienced things on my own, so I know what is real. If believing in angels makes me happy and a better person then why would you be upset with me?"

"I am not upset with you," Dave said, trying to keep his patience intact.

"You sound upset," Anna said in a quiet voice.

"Look, this is crazy stuff. It really is. However, your mother and grandmother have indoctrinated you, so I guess I can't do anything about it. I just wanted to warn you of what may lie ahead if you keep this up. You are my daughter too, you know."

"Yes, Dad, I appreciate your concern. I really do, but I am happy and I believe in the things I have experienced as signs from my angels. If it makes you feel better, it has made me feel closer to God. I like knowing that God sent angels with me when I was born, and they will stay with me until I pass over. I like having them to talk to and give me help. It has helped me understand what a loving God does for his children. Besides, I haven't stopped going to church, nor have I joined some strange group. I'm still the same, only maybe more aware of things."

"Okay, I have said what I needed to say. I know it didn't make a difference, but I had to say it. I want you to be happy and you are. That's what I care about. I still wish you wouldn't expose yourself to criticism by doing readings. I don't believe in it, and I think it will just lead to trouble. I will continue to worry about you, and if you need a shoulder to cry on, use mine. We'll get together soon. I'll call you next week. I have a big account coming up so maybe you can ask your angels to assist me if they've got the time." He laughed at his little joke. He wanted to end on a light note with Anna.

"Thanks, Dad. I love you."

"Me, too," her dad said gently as he hung up the phone.

Anna didn't like having her dad upset with her, but she felt their conversation had gone pretty well. She had remained calm and explained herself. Her dad seemed to accept what she had to say even if he didn't like it. She should have told him how she didn't like all the attention and that some kids did think she was weird. What she really wanted was to keep her angel work very quiet so people would move on to another topic.

Chapter 10

Christmas break ended and classes resumed. Semester exams were approaching and everyone was trying to remember a semester's worth of knowledge. Students grouped together in study groups, and Thom and Anna were together frequently. Mark, Maddie, Anna, and Thom all went bowling the night after being at Mark's house. That was the beginning of Anna and Thom's romance. Anna remembered the romance card she had drawn and thanked her angels that their predictions came true.

Anna was needed at her mother's shop as much now as during Christmas. The construction on the addition was right on schedule, so a pre-Valentine Day opening was being planned. Karen had been able to stock angel reading cards before Christmas, and they were a popular Christmas gift. Anna hosted a couple angel gatherings at her house, and Karen showed the girls how to use their cards. This allowed Anna to step into the background and let her mother become the angel expert. Anna was getting to know a lot of new people and was surprised how the angel interest crossed over the school cliques. Preps, jocks, Goths, nerds, artists—it didn't matter; someone from each group showed an interest. It was pretty cool to see kids come together like that when at school they stayed apart. Now people actually said hello to someone who was in different social group. They would never sit at the same cafeteria table, but now they at least acknowledged each other's presence. Anna decided this was a good thing.

Things were good in Anna's life if she didn't count her dwindling friendship with Maddie. After the school lunch when Anna was surrounded by her angel friends, Maddie had made it a point to never discuss angels with Anna. She had no interest in the cards or going to an angel party with the other girls. However, Anna was hoping Maddie would meet Mary Matson at the store's opening. Mary had agreed to give an angel workshop as part of the opening of the addition featuring the gorgeous angel fountain.

"Do you think you'll be able to come to the shop and meet Mary?" asked Anna when she and Maddie were walking in the hall together after school.

"I don't think so," Maddie answered evasively.

"Why not? You never want to do anything anymore." Anna was clearly frustrated.

"All you ever do is talk about angels. You have a lot of angel girls who worship the ground you walk on. I just don't care to be one of them," Maddie said angrily.

"I don't talk about angels around you. I can't. You act like you are jealous, which is totally ridiculous," Anna said accusingly.

Both girls had stopped walking and were glaring at each other. The halls were empty and their voices sounded especially loud in the hall.

"I'm not jealous. I just think all this angel stuff has gone to your head, and you've changed. That's what is ridiculous!" Maddie said angrily.

"How have I changed?"

"You are too nice! You never say anything mean about anyone anymore. And you are always so positive about everything! It's sickening. It's like you swallowed a giant sugar cube. You just aren't normal. However ... I am glad you were nice enough to introduce me to Mark. He is absolutely awesome," Maddie said as her tone and face softened. Her eyes appeared to glazed over.

"Is there something going on between you and Mark?" Anna looked at Maddie, wondering what Maddie was up to. First, she was almost yelling, and then she was cooing like a dove.

"Mark and I realized we really clicked after being together, so we have talked to each other every day since he went back to Cincinnati. We text each other constantly! We're really getting close," Maddie said demurely, twisting a strand of hair.

Maddie looked like a cat that had captured its prey. *What's this all about?* Anna was perplexed. Maddie always got the guy she wanted. What made Mark such a trophy?

"I've also had a chance to get to know Lauren," Maddie said as she gave Anna a sideways glance. "I know how you feel about her, but she's been nice to me."

Here it comes: the famous knife in the back, and from my best friend! Anna thought feeling certain there was more to come.

Maddie continued but wouldn't look directly at Anna. "Mom had some questions about some medicine she was taking, so I asked Mark if I could talk to Lauren about it. It really is handy having a pharmacist we can talk to. She said to not hesitate to call. She was really cool with me, Anna. Maybe you need to use some of your angel sweetness on Lauren."

Anna was beginning to boil. "I am nice to Lauren. She doesn't choose to reciprocate. She has my dad chained to her side and heart. And now, she has you. How nice!"

"Oh, Anna, come on. Get over it! You have complained about Lauren ever since your dad married her. Since I never knew her until now, of course I sided with you. Now I'm beginning to think you just don't like her because she took your dad away,"

Maddie said in her lecturing tone. "Haven't they been married long enough now that you could act a little more mature and give her a chance?"

Anna stared at Maddie in disbelief. An alien from the planet Lauren had taken over Maddie's body. Her voice was the same, but the words coming from her mouth were someone else's. "Sure, Maddie, you're right. You had one conversation with Lauren, and now she is your new best friend. I'm wrong and Lauren is a sweet and lovable woman, not the witch I've made her out to be. How could I have been so blind to all the goodness that oozes from this wonderful, benevolent being?" said Anna sarcastically.

"All I can say is that she has been nice to me. And I've talked to her more than once. One night I was struggling with calculus, and she got on the phone and talked me through the problem. She was an excellent teacher. She was so patient and explained everything so clearly. Obviously you have issues with her, but I like her." Maddie spoke with an air of superiority. It was as if there had been a contest over Lauren and Maddie had won.

"I need to go. I have to get to the shop." Anna's eyes were clouded with tears as she hurriedly left school. She didn't know what to say to Maddie. Her best friend had mutated into something she didn't understand. *She enjoyed hurting me. Why?* Anna thought. She was trying to avoid the icy patches on the sidewalk when something caught her eye. She bent over for a closer look; it was someone's earring. She had hoped for a penny. *I guess there won't always be pennies.* She brushed off the light snow and put it in her pocket. *It doesn't matter; I know I'm not alone. Angels, stay with me. Maddie has gone to Lauren's side; better known as the dark side. They deserve each other! I'm done with both of them. I don't care!* Anna was furious with Maddie and hurt, and she really did care.

"I find solace in my books." Anna thought about what her grandmother had written as she unpacked books at the shop. The angel fountain would be the focal piece of the store's addition. In one corner there would be the hot tea, and the inspirational items would be on the right as customers entered the fountain area. The room wasn't very large, but the high, sunlit ceiling made it appear open and welcoming. Right now, Anna was drawn to the books.

"You can't control anyone's feeling but your own," she read as she thumbed through one of the books. She recognized the author from her research. She knew when she got home she would go to her grandmother's journals. There was something she remembered reading about not accepting someone else's anger. "Easier said than done," she mused.

Karen never let Anna work past 7:30 p.m.; she needed to get her homework done and get to bed on time. When she got home, Anna made herself a cup of apple herbal tea and then went to her grandmother's room. She settled into her grandmother's rocking chair with three journals on her lap. She remembered reading some steps her grandmother had written about resolving conflict. *I think it is in this blue, flowered one,* she thought as she carefully turned the pages and read her grandmother's words.

Authors make forgiving someone sound easier than it is. Pray, meditate on releasing anger, pray, etc. Words hurt! Every time I replay the tape of harsh words in my head, I hurt again. Maybe that should be step one. Don't keep replaying the tape!

Steps to Forgive

1. Wounds can't heal if you continue to pick at them.

2. Examine self. How did my actions contribute to the problem? (Ouch!)

3. Speak and listen with an open heart in solving the problem.

4. Pray for strength, understanding, and willingness to forgive.

5. Love; those who aren't loving need love the most! (and patience)

Anna sat and reread this entry. She saw herself in her grandma's words. She replayed Maddie's words over and over in her head, and now her insides felt bruised. Anna decided she should catch herself and say a prayer rather than replay the hurtful conversation. *I'll work at this*, she thought. Grandma had warned her about picking scabs. She had never thought about emotional wounds having scabs.

Two days passed without Anna and Maddie speaking. Maddie didn't go to lunch and avoided her in the halls. Anna continued saying her prayer of understanding, and once she stopped burning internally, she was able to think about Maddie and what may have contributed to her nastiness. *Maddie clearly didn't like my new friendships. She also thought communicating with angels was crazy. We have agreed on just about everything up until now, so it's no wonder Maddie is mad at me. I have changed, and she doesn't understand*, Anna thought. *I don't want to lose Maddie's friendship; we've been friends too long to not overcome this. I'll talk to her and tell her how important her friendship is to me. She probably feels hurt and left out, so she hurt me. I think I get it!* Anna felt better after reading what her grandmother had written. She believed she could solve the Maddie problem with some work.

On Sunday, Anna called Maddie. It had been four days since Maddie had vented her feelings to Anna. Anna was nervous as she pressed Maddie's number. Maddie answered on the third ring.

"Hi, Anna! Guess where I am?" Maddie said happily.

Anna was surprised by Maddie's cheerful greeting. "I don't know, where?" Anna asked tentatively.

"I'm at your dad's house with Mark. I guess I should say Mark's house now," giggled Maddie.

"Oh. Well, tell Mark hi. Is my dad there?" Anna spoke haltingly.

"No, just Mark and Lauren. Mark is saying you should come over. Do you want to, or are you too busy?" asked Maddie, not encouraging the invite.

"I can't. I'm at work, but I thought maybe we could get a pizza together or something tonight. Mom is working herself to death trying to get everything ready for the opening, so she won't be home until late, and I haven't seen you for a while." Anna was struggling with what to say.

"I know; I have been swamped. Those teachers just keep piling the work on. They don't realize we have lives outside of school."

"What about tonight? Do you think you can meet me for dinner?" asked Anna.

"I don't know. I'll check with Mom and get back to you," said Maddie. "Hey, Mark wants to talk to you."

"Hi! Just wanted you to know I'll be at school tomorrow. Maddie is picking me up in the morning, which is cool. Thom said he'd show me around once I got there. It sure makes this easier knowing a few people. Thanks for introducing me," Mark said.

"No problem. I'm glad it helped. Listen, I've got to get back to work. Tell Maddie to let me know about tonight. See you tomorrow," Anna said before hanging up. She was still getting used to the way Maddie acted around Mark. It was beyond strange. Maddie had never been one of those girls who got all wrapped up in a guy. The guys were the ones who became a little unglued around her. Maddie usually had control of the relationship, so she never acted goofy over a guy. Now she was simpering over Mark, and it made Anna a little nauseous.

A few minutes later Maddie sent Anna a text. It said: "I have to be home for Sunday dinner, but I'll meet you at Duval's for coffee at 7:30 if that works."

"See ya then," answered Anna. She was looking forward to seeing her friend. She'd been focusing on their friendship and had done a good job of releasing her hurt feelings. It wasn't easy, but she certainly felt better than she had four days ago.

There was a little awkwardness between the girls when they first sat down at a table together. They each ordered their usuals. Anna loved café mochas, and Maddie always had a skinny latte. Duval's huge cookies were large enough to split, so they ordered a raisin oatmeal cookie to share. Anna began. "Did my dad show up today?"

"Yes, right before I left. He said it was funny seeing me without you at my side. I told him I was seeing you tonight, and he said to tell you to call him when you get home this evening," chirped Maddie, happy as a little bird.

"I've never seen you like this before. You have really flipped over Mark, haven't you?"

"I have. He is so awesome. I am sooo happy he's here in Sweet Grove now. I can hardly wait until tomorrow to show him off. I'm especially looking forward to seeing Suzanne Hopkins's face when I walk into school with him tomorrow," Maddie said triumphantly.

"Suzanne won't care. She's crazy about Kevin. Haven't you seen them together?"

"Are you really that naïve? What has happened to you? Suzanne always has to have the hottest guy in school. Well, the hottest guy in school is now Mark! It won't be long before she tries to get her claws into him," Maddie said nastily.

"I used to think Suzanne was like that, but I don't anymore. I've gotten to know her because she came to an angel party, and we've continued to talk since then. I think she's really nice."

"You are really too much," Maddie said exasperated with Anna.

"Why? Because I don't agree with you about someone?"

"We have gone to school with Suzanne since sixth grade. She has always gone from one guy to the next. 'Love and Leave 'Em' Suzanne, remember? I can't believe that because she is now an angel convert she has changed her dating pattern. There is no way she won't make a play for Mark. I'll give it two weeks before she begins."

Anna sat looking at Maddie. Maddie seemed more interested in having Mark to strut around with than actually being with him. She knew Maddie was crazy about him, but even so, it bothered her that Maddie considered him a trophy. It's funny how Maddie disliked Suzanne for going from one boy to the next when Maddie had always done the exact same thing. Sticking up for Suzanne had not helped the evening's plan of mending their friendship. Anna didn't want to argue. She wanted her best friend to be her best friend again.

"I don't want to talk about Suzanne. I just want to hear about you and have fun together like we used to."

"Anna, I have to be honest with you. It's been really hard on me seeing you change so much. I have to admit, I just don't like it. Ever since you did that angel report and became a Sweet Grove superstar, you act differently. I can't talk to you the way I used to. I feel like you are sitting in judgment of me because I'm not an angel freak. It's hard to have fun with you anymore."

"Look, I don't care if you are into angels or not. And by the way, we are not freaks. Just because I don't agree with you about someone doesn't mean I'm judging you. You're entitled to your opinion, and I'm entitled to mine. I was hoping that we'd work out our differences tonight, not create new ones," Anna said, trying to keep the conversation on a healing path.

"You're right. You are not an angel freak. I'm sorry. We do need to iron out our problems, because it will really be difficult on Mark if we don't get along," said Maddie.

"Mark has nothing to do with our friendship, or lack of. You really have gone over the edge," Anna said, putting her hand on her forehead and slowly shaking her head.

"Of course he has something to do with our friendship. He is your stepbrother and my boyfriend, so that makes us almost related. Therefore, we are required to get along. I've always acted like a big sister to you anyway."

"What are you talking about?" asked Anna totally lost.

"You know how over the years I have given you advice on your clothes, makeup, and hair style. For example, the haircut you have now was my idea. And I have warned you about certain people to watch out for. You have always been a little naïve, so it has been my job to kinda protect and advise you." Maddie was so arrogant and full of herself that Anna had to take a deep breath and wait before she responded.

"The only people I can think of that you warned me about were guys that I liked that you also liked. As if I would be any threat! As for my hair, I showed you a picture, and you agreed it was the perfect cut. It's not like you went out of your way trying to find the perfect hairstyle for me." Anna could not believe what she was hearing. As far as she was concerned, they had just been friends. She hadn't realized that she had been a personal project for Maddie. She had never thought of Maddie as her advisor; Maddie had just been her friend.

"Maddie, I thought we were friends. You make me sound like I've been your little charity case or something."

"Don't be ridiculous!" Maddie's blue eyes were blazing.

Anna began slowly. "It all makes sense now. This is the first time I've received more attention than you. I have always been in the background when it came to your popularity, and I have liked being there. Yeah, you like me; what's not to like? I follow your lead in everything. Until now; now I have my own identity. I am not a Maddie shadow person. That's how I've changed. People noticed me instead of you." As Anna spoke, she saw Maddie bristle.

"Anna, the snow is really coming down now; I think we should go," Maddie said as she stood and wrapped her red wool scarf around her neck.

"Maddie, please, we need to finish this. We have been friends for too long to be acting like this. Remember we said nothing could break us apart? Just another few minutes won't matter with the roads." A voice in Anna's head was saying, *Send her love, be patient, let her know you value her friendship.* "You have been my friend through some of my toughest times. Like when Grandma died. I agree that I have changed. I have found something that I believe in that has helped me and can help others. I like knowing I have God's angels with me. I also like knowing I have friends I can count on. You don't have to be an angel convert to be my friend, but you have to be able to accept that I will be with girls who share my interest in angels. Our friendship is based on years of experiences and growing up together. Just because we don't share this doesn't mean our friendship is over, I hope. There's more to me than that! Please, Maddie, we have to try." Anna's voice shook and her eyes filled with tears as she looked at Maddie.

"Anna, of course we are still going to be friends. I believe at the beginning of this conversation I stated that we needed to find a way to iron at our differences, remember? I think our little talk has helped us understand each other better. Now, we really need to go. Look outside; it's piling up," Maddie said as she pulled on her heavy coat and gloves.

"Maybe we'll have a snow day tomorrow," Anna said hopefully. "If we do, do you want to come over?"

"If we do, maybe we could go sledding on Urlin Hill with Mark and Thom," Maddie said smiling brightly.

"Now that's something we can agree on!" said Anna with a laugh, and the girls entered the white evening feeling that their friendship still had a chance.

Chapter 11

"**M**addie is the nicest and prettiest girl Mark has ever dated," Lauren happily chirped as she prepared dinner. Anna was helping Lauren in the kitchen and was trying her hardest to be pleasant to Lauren. "You're lucky to have her for a friend."

"Yes, I am," Anna responded in a flat tone of voice.

"She's very talented too. I'm looking forward to seeing her in *My Fair Lady*. You're in it too, right?"

"Yes, we both made it," agreed Anna as she collected silverware for the table.

"Since she is Eliza Doolittle, she will be incredibly busy learning her lines and songs. Being the lead, the success of the show falls on her shoulders." Lauren was clearly impressed with Maddie.

"Lauren, the entire cast will be working hard to make this a great show. We will all be busy. If we aren't on stage, we're working on sets. The stars get out of the set work, and there is a lot to be done."

"You sound a little envious of your friend. I'm sure what you're doing is just as important, and I know you'll do a fine job in the chorus." Lauren couldn't help but sound more than a little condescending.

Anna refrained from throwing a hot roll at Lauren's head. "I'll go tell Mark and Dad dinner's ready," she said as she left the kitchen. *Be patient, be patient*, she told herself as she twisted the dish towel in her hand.

"Come on, dinner's ready," Anna said when she found her Dad and Mark sitting in front of the new big screen TV. "Sports, sports, sports, don't you ever watch anything else?"

"Only if I have to," laughed Anna's dad.

"What if the only sport on TV was fishing, would you watch it?" asked Anna.

"It's a sport, isn't it?" Dave said, putting his arm around his daughter and giving her a squeeze. The only thing that makes a sport better is if it is an Ohio State team. There is nothing like cheering on the Buckeyes!"

"Dad, you're crazy," Anna said as she shook her head. "I'll never understand how a Buckeye can be a team mascot. Mascots are supposed to be ferocious animals."

"Anna, my dear," Dave said, giving her a squeeze, "buckeyes are a poisonous nut. That makes them fearful."

"Oh, I see. Teams should be afraid of a nut who wears a sweater, because if someone would lick him, they might get sick. It makes perfect sense."

"I'm glad you understand. Being a Buckeye fan is required if you have dinner here, so act like you are one," Dave said laughing.

She loved being with her father. Dinner tonight would have been great if Lauren wasn't there.

"Thanks for helping Mark get adjusted. He said you've been a big help, Anna," Dave said as he sat down to the table. "Prime rib! Wow! I thought you said we were having meatloaf?" Dave said, looking at Lauren.

"I wanted you to be surprised," Lauren said as she kissed her husband's cheek. "This is the first dinner the four of us have had since Christmas, and I wanted to make it special."

"If you have cherry pie for dessert, then it is perfect," Dave said.

"Well, then it is perfect, because I do," said Lauren cheerfully. "How is school, you two?"

"Fine," Mark and Anna answered in unison.

"Valentine's Day is two weeks away. Is there going to be a dance?" asked Lauren, looking at Mark.

"Yes, and before you ask, yes, I'm going with Maddie," Mark said while stabbing a huge piece of beef.

"She'll be the prettiest girl there, I'm sure," Lauren said without thinking.

"You mean one of the prettiest girls there," said Anna's father trying to smooth over Lauren's comment. "I bet this will cost me a new dress; won't it, Anna?"

"Mom already bought me a dress, Dad."

"I could buy the shoes. I know all about shoes having to go with the dress," offered Dave.

"Thanks, Dad, but it's covered," said Anna quietly. She was totally uncomfortable and was no longer hungry. The meal that had looked so delicious just a few minutes ago now looked disgusting.

"Hey, I heard some of the girls talking about your mom's shop today. Is there some speaker coming next Saturday?" asked Mark.

"Yes, Mom has a speaker coming in connection with the opening of the shop's addition. She's going all out for this," Anna said proudly.

"Who's the speaker?" asked Lauren.

"Mary Matson."

"Really? I saw her new book at the bookstore. That's quite an accomplishment for your mom to get her to come to a small community like Sweet Grove," Lauren said, clearly impressed.

"Mom couldn't believe her luck. I'm sure there will be a big turnout. Mom has been working herself to death trying to get everything ready. The only time I see her is when I'm at work too. I just hope we aren't hit by another snowstorm!"

"I wish I could hear Mary Matson. I should have bought her book. I've been so busy with the house that I knew I wouldn't have time to read," Lauren said, and she looked at Anna for a response.

Anna waited. *I don't want her there! Please, please, don't make me ask her.* Anna's thoughts were racing. *There's no way out of this, is there?* "I guess you could come if you really want to. Like I said, we expect a big crowd." *You can get lost in the crowd, and I won't have to deal with you,* Anna thought.

"Being new in town, it would be nice to have you there to introduce me to some people. I especially want to meet Mary," Lauren said.

I'm doomed, thought Anna gloomily.

"Lauren, do you really think this is a good idea? I don't like the idea of you going to my ex-wife's store, and you know how I feel about this angel stuff," Dave said, clearly agitated by the idea.

"Anna, will your mother care if I come?" Lauren tilted her head and put on her little girl innocent face.

No, she is glad you have to deal with dad instead of her. I'm the one who cares, she thought. Anna said, "Mom, won't care."

"I suppose you'll be busy too, but maybe Maddie will introduce me to her mom and some other mothers."

"Actually, Maddie won't be there, but I'm pretty sure her mother will," said Anna carefully.

"Oh! Why isn't Maddie coming? Is she just too busy to fit one more thing in? I sure know how that is," Lauren said knowingly.

"Lauren, Maddie doesn't want to come. She is no busier than I am. In fact, she isn't as busy. She doesn't have a part-time job, you know," Anna said, trying not to let her irritation show.

"I'm concerned that you're doing too much," Dave interjected. "I hope you'll cut back at the store now that you're rehearsing for the musical. You can't afford to let your grades slip."

"Mom and I have it all worked out, Dad. I can handle it," said Anna.

"I could talk to Maddie about coming if you want me to," offered Lauren. "We've developed a nice relationship."

I am going to throw up. "That really won't be necessary. Thanks. You just come. I'll introduce you to a few people, and it'll be fine." Changing the subject, she said, "It's getting late; I should be going. I still have homework to do. Thanks for dinner." Anna hurriedly took her plate to the sink and got her coat from the closet. Her dad walked her to the door.

"What's going on with Maddie? Does Mark have anything to do with it?" asked her dad.

"No, Dad, nothing is going on. Maddie just isn't into angels." She hugged her Dad and said ruefully, "You know about not being into angels, right?"

"I sure do. I'd just hate to see you lose Maddie as a friend over something as ridiculous as angels," Dave said, looking intently at his daughter.

"Dad, this is important to me. I think people who love me shouldn't criticize my interests just because they don't share them. Isn't that, right?" Anna said firmly, returning her father's look.

"I just want what's best for you. If this crazy angel stuff makes you happy, then go for it. I do love you, even if I don't say it enough. You've always been my little angel," Anna's dad said affectionately.

"Thanks, Dad. I love you too. Maybe just the two of us could go to dinner sometime like we used to. Wouldn't that be fun?"

Dave looked at his daughter thoughtfully and said, "I would like to have Lauren there so the two of you can spend time together. It's important that we include her in our plans. She would feel hurt if she thought you didn't want her."

"Whatever you say, Dad. You're the boss." Anna's chest felt like it had been punched as she managed a weak smile. Just once she wanted to come first with her dad!

Chapter 12

"I am so happy to be here in this beautiful setting. Hasn't Karen done a wonderful job?" Mary Matson's question was answered by loud applause. She was a small woman with brown hair and large brown eyes. She wore black slacks and a blue sweater, and she had a warm smile and sweet face that shown from an inner light. Her voice was soft and her laugh was light and cheerful. Mary was like a little, round fairy.

"I know you all came to hear about angels and to learn how to communicate with yours, but I need to tell you why angels are so important to me. I am a Christian, but angels do not belong to any one faith. Many faiths acknowledge angels. That is one of the best things about angels; people of different faiths can come together and agree that God sends angels to help us humans. Isn't that fantastic?" Mary beamed as she spoke. "My hope is that each of you will leave today knowing that you have loving angels around you, and therefore, you will feel closer to God. That is the purpose of my work. I am happy to be your angelic teacher. Let's get started."

Anna looked around the room and found her mother seated by the angel fountain.

She looked so happy and at ease. The stress of getting ready for Mary's arrival seemed to have been washed away. The room was filled with teenagers and women of all ages. A few men were in attendance along with a couple of teenage boys. Their goal was most likely to please the women in their lives. Lauren was seated with Maddie's mother and some other moms. Lauren seemed nervous when she arrived, but Anna quickly introduced her to a few people and she relaxed. It was funny to see Lauren unsure of herself.

"Many, many books have been written about angels appearing as humans. Angels have comforted the sick in hospitals, pulled children from ponds, and prevented countless tragedies. I can't tell you why some tragedies are prevented and some are not. However, I'm thankful for those that are.

"There are many different ways people know their angels are with them. The smell of flowers, particularly roses, is one way. Some people can feel their angels' presence, and others can hear angelic voices. I know quite a few people who can see angels. When you begin communicating with your angels, it is usually by asking for signs or using angel cards. Writing your questions down is a good way to be sure you are clear in what you are asking. You can have someone else read angel cards for you, but I think it is important to work at establishing a personal relationship with your angels. It is always good to have a mentor, but with patience and practice, you'll be having regular chats with your angelic friends.

"I want to make the most of our short time together, so you will be going to one of two stations. My friend Stephanie will be at station one, showing how to use angel cards and how to receive answers by using a pendulum. I will be at station two for those who have been working on communicating with their angels for a while. This group is for those who are already familiar with the cards and the pendulum. I too am a student and would like to hear what some of you have done in your angel work. Each one of us is unique in our thoughts and the ways we communicate with each other and our angelic friends. Keep that in mind as you try different techniques. My group will be in this back area, and Stephanie's group will be in the front by the cards and books. I will lead both groups through a meditation exercise in preparation for our work. Five minutes and we begin!" Mary said happily.

Anna, along with Suzanne and some of her other friends, were in Mary's group. They had bought cards and learned how to use them from Anna's mother. She had also showed them how to ask a yes or no question and receive an answer by using a pendulum. Lauren was in the other group, and Karen was not in either group. She was here to assist Mary in any way that was needed. Anna was able to completely relax and open her mind as she listened to the music and Mary's calming voice.

"Please select someone you don't know as a partner. It would be nice if you and your partner are different ages. Sit facing each other and take each other's hands. Close your eyes and just simply feel the other person's presence. Breathe, relax, and be open to receiving. Ask to receive any messages that would help your partner," Mary directed.

Anna partnered with a woman who was in her mid-thirties. She had curly red hair, bright blue eyes, and one large dimple in her left cheek. Her name was Sophie. They took each other's hands and closed their eyes. It couldn't have been longer than a minute when Anna felt the tingling. Anna opened her eyes and asked, "Did you feel that?"

"Yes. It was a tingling sensation. I'm taking it as a good sign. Let's try again. I'll ask about you first, okay?"

"That'd be great," Anna replied, not eager to go first.

After a few minutes, Sophie opened her eyes and smiled and said, "I saw a hummingbird, and I sensed the presence of an older man. I couldn't see him clearly, but the hummingbird was clear."

Anna opened her eyes and whispered, "That is my grandfather."

"I can't believe I saw anything, but I did. This is amazing!" exclaimed Sophie.

"What is the connection of a hummingbird to your grandfather?"

"His angels would send him hummingbirds as a sign that they were with him. He knew that if you saw hummingbirds I would know he was here. Thank you," Anna said gratefully.

"Are you ready to give it a try and ask about me?"

"I'm ready," Anna said. Once again the two clasped hands, closed their eyes, and asked for a message for Sophie.

It seemed to Anna she was sitting for a long time. She told herself to relax and asked again and waited. Bright colors of blues, greens, and purples filled her head. Anna was filled with a sense of peace and love. When the colors faded, she saw a beautiful figure that seemed to glow and shimmer. She heard a voice say, "You are on the right path." Anna waited before opening her eyes. "I think I saw an angel," she whispered. "There were all these colors and then a shimmering figure spoke." Anna was shaking her head as if to clear her head.

Sophie reached over and hugged Anna. "I have been praying and praying for a sign. What did the angel say?"

Anna carefully repeated what the angel said.

Sophie thanked Anna with tears in her eyes. "I have been struggling with a decision, and I have been afraid of making a mistake. This is what I came here for." Sophie didn't explain what decision she had been struggling with, but Anna knew she had received her answer.

Mary picked up a set of hand chimes and gently ran her fingers across them. The tinkling of the chimes signaled that the groups needed to come together. The two separate groups became one again and Mary spoke.

"One of the best parts of a workshop is the sharing of what I like to call the 'I can't believe what just happened moments.' Would anyone like to share?"

A woman who had been using angel cards raised her hand and spoke. "I came here with my sister, and I had my doubts about all this," she said as she motioned with her hand, "But Heather pulled five cards, and each card had meaning for me. I just met Heather, so she didn't know the significance of the cards as she read their messages. I have to admit there is something to all this angel hoopla," she said with a laugh, and she shook her head like she was having difficulty believing.

"How did you feel, Heather?" asked Mary.

"I thought it was pretty cool that Julie understood what each card meant. When it was her turn to read the cards for me, I knew the meaning of three, but I wasn't sure about the other two," explained Heather.

"I'm glad you said that because sometimes the card won't have significance until later. Something will happen, and then you'll think back to the card and know what it meant. The cards can refer to past, present, or future. The broader the question is the broader the answer is. For example, a common question a reader might ask is, 'What would you like me to know about this person?' That is so broad; all kinds of information can come in. Asking the question, 'What does the next six months hold for this person?' is a much clearer question, and the answer will be easier to understand. Would anyone else like to share?" Mary asked, looking around the room.

Anna's friend Suzanne raised her hand. She had been in the same group as Anna. "My partner and I both saw an item that the other person would recognize. I saw a package of Camel cigarettes, and Teri saw an umbrella stand with a ladybug umbrella on it. Teri's grandfather smoked Camels, and my grandmother had an umbrella stand in her foyer. When I was about seven, Grandma bought me a ladybug umbrella that I played with every time I visited. I just met Teri today. I never thought anything like this could happen. I still don't understand how we could know these things about each other, but that's what we saw," Suzanne said.

"You were both open to receiving. Our deceased loved ones keep a watchful eye on us. If we are in need, they are around to support us. Deceased loved ones seem to be eager to let their families know they are near when I have these workshops. More people hear from loved ones than they do angels at my workshops. I can't explain why. Did anyone see an angel or feel its presence?" Mary asked the group.

Three hands went up. An older woman said she smelled flowers and saw a swirl of bright colors. A young girl of about thirteen said she saw a figure surrounded by a green light. Mary said that the girl's partner might have needed to heal something in her life since she had seen a lot of green.

"Green is a color of healing. When you meditate, picture yourself in a field of green, healing grass. Breathe in the freshness and allow the healing energy to pass through your body. Exhale any anger or bitterness you feel. It is amazing how well this works! Try it and see for yourself.

"Our angels provide what we need if we ask for their help. We must ask though. Since we all have free will, angels can't interfere in our lives without an invitation. If you have an argument with someone, try mentally surrounding them in green and ask for healing. You'll be surprised at the results. I think Anna had her hand up. Anna, did you see an angel?"

Anna was a little self-conscious about sharing. This was all new territory, and she wasn't sure how to handle the terrain. "I think it was an angel. I heard her speak. She had a message for my partner, so it had to be an angel. It's hard to describe what it was like." Anna was still moved by the deep love she had felt from the angel.

Mary gave Anna a joyful smile and continued. "There have been so many wonderful spiritual experiences today that I wish we had more time to share. Please continue to share with each other over the next few weeks. It's the sharing that brings and holds us together. I hope you will share email addresses so you can continue to find support. I can remember trying to tell someone about receiving a sign from my angels and being laughed at. I knew it was real, but my happiness was diminished by my friend's disbelief. Having someone who can appreciate your joyful experiences is very important.

"Our time together has come to an end, and I want to thank all of you for coming and participating. It is always fun for me to share what I know and see the excitement of people discovering their spiritual capabilities. Blessings to you all, and please come to Karen's store frequently!"

People quickly began finding their friends and eagerly shared their experiences. New acquaintances exchanged telephone numbers and email addresses. Suzanne was headed for Anna, but Lauren got to her first.

"You are very fortunate to have seen and actually heard an angel today," Lauren said with a nasty, suspicious tone. "Isn't it amazing that you not only saw an angel, but you heard her speak?"

"What are you saying? Are you trying to imply that I made it up?" Anna said, clearly upset.

"Well, this is your mother's shop, and Mary is your mother's friend. It is just such a coincidence that you'd be the one to receive angelic information," Lauren said smugly as if she had figured out a devious plot.

Anna shook her head and tried to swallow her anger. "Lauren, many people received messages today. I was not the only one. You can't really believe I would pretend something like that. I wouldn't even know how to."

Lauren looked at Anna, a little less sure of herself now. "Well, perhaps I am wrong, but it is quite a coincidence. I couldn't see or hear anything. I tried. I really did. But nothing happened. I apparently wasn't doing it right," she said with her familiar pout.

Anna was trying to be patient with Lauren. "I don't know why I was able to receive and you weren't. Maybe it is because I didn't have any doubts that I could."

"So are you saying that I wasn't trying?" asked Lauren defensively.

"No, but maybe you were trying too hard. I just totally relaxed and believed that if there was something I was supposed to know, it would come through," explained Anna. "I'm guessing that you were nervous and afraid that you couldn't do it."

"Of course I was nervous! It's not every day I ask advice from angels! Having Mary's friend Stephanie as my partner made me more nervous," Lauren whined.

"You had Stephanie? Wow, you were lucky," Anna said, impressed.

"You think so? I think I would have been better off with someone who wasn't an expert. It was intimidating, and you're right, I was a nervous wreck."

"Okay, but you were reading cards in your group. Did Stephanie understand the meanings of the cards you put down for her?" wondered Anna.

"Well, of course she did! She knows everything!" Lauren said too loudly.

"Then you were successful. I think if I'm guided to lay down meaningful cards then I have been a success. Didn't you feel that way?" asked Anna.

"Yes, I guess. But I'm not talking about the cards. After Stephanie showed us how to use the pendulum, and we each read cards for our partner, we took each other's hands like your group did. That's where I was a total failure. All I saw was the back of my eyelids!" complained Lauren.

"I probably would have been intimidated too. What did she tell you?" asked Anna, eager to hear.

"It's personal, and let's just say I didn't like what she said she saw in my near future." Lauren couldn't say anymore because Maddie's mother came up to say good-bye.

"It was so nice to meet you, Lauren. I really appreciate all the help you gave me with my medication. It is nice to know a pharmacist. I'm at the grocery all the time, so I'll stop by the pharmacy and say hello when I'm there. Wasn't this a wonderful afternoon?" Maddie's mother, Beth, said enthusiastically.

"It really was. And I'm so happy that Anna was so successful today. Of course, her father thinks she's an angel already, so why wouldn't she be able to see and hear from one?" laughed Lauren easily.

Anna looked at Lauren in shock. Lauren had been transformed into a new human being. *How does she do that? She attacks me and five minutes later she compliments me. I will never, ever understand this woman. She is so different from Mom. How could Dad have two such different wives?* Anna wondered for the hundredth time since her dad married Lauren.

"Anna has always been a sweetie. I'm grateful that she and Maddie are so close. I understand that Anna has been working on communicating with angels for some time, so that gives me confidence that I too will be rewarded if I keep trying. I need to run; my friend is waiting for me. I know I will see you again soon, Lauren." Beth gave Anna a quick hug and left.

Beth nor Anna had mentioned Maddie not coming today. Anna was curious what Maddie had said to her mom about Anna and her angel stuff. Being friends for so long meant that Anna was also close to Maddie's family. *Why couldn't Dad have married someone like Maddie's mom? There are a lot of women I can think of that would have been a better choice. This is so crazy having to see Lauren on a regular basis. I can't believe she is really interested in angels. It just doesn't fit her personality!* Anna thought as she stood with Lauren and watched Maddie's mom say good-bye.

Chapter 13

It was obvious that Suzanne was waiting to talk to Anna, so Anna excused herself from Lauren.

"Mary asked me to find you. She wants to talk to you about the angel group you started at school," Suzanne said excitedly.

Anna was nervous as she walked over to Mary. She wondered what Mary had heard. She didn't like being seen as some angel guru, because she wasn't.

"Suzanne was telling me about the angel group you started at school. It looks like there was a lot of interest from the turnout we had today. I think more than half of the people here today were teenagers. I'm impressed," said Mary.

"I really didn't get the group going. Suzanne did. All I did was a research project on angels, and things sort of spiraled from there," Anna said self-consciously.

"After her research project, Anna read angel cards for people and showed several of us how to use them. Of course, Anna's mom also taught us a lot about angels, but Anna was the one who got it started." Suzanne was eager to share how she had learned to communicate with her angels.

"I have never had so many teenagers at one of my workshops before. It makes me realize that I need to do more to make teenagers feel welcome and want to attend. You girls must be the reason so many were here today," Mary said with her famous sweet smile.

"I think they came because Mom sold the cards and taught so many of them at our house," Anna said, not wanting the credit for the girls coming. She was glad her mom had taken over the teaching. When the girls came to her house, it was just like she was one of them. She liked not being the expert.

"Weren't you also teaching?" asked Mary.

"I did a little, but it was mostly Mom," Anna replied.

Suzanne was quick to interject. "Anna doesn't like to admit all she did. She taught me. She taught a lot of us. I agree there were so many teens here today because of Anna, and maybe a little because of me. Anna is so cool because her belief in being able to receive divine guidance is so strong. When she teaches, she is confident that anyone can receive if they want to. As her student, her confidence rubbed off on me." Suzanne smiled warmly at Anna.

Anna just stood there and couldn't think of anything to say.

"I'm thinking that I could use a couple teenage assistants. What do you think? Would you two be willing to come and help me at a workshop in Cincinnati? I'll have to get you the date. It will begin on a Friday night and conclude on Sunday around noon," explained Mary.

Suzanne quickly volunteered, but Anna wasn't so sure. "I don't know. I'll have to think about it. It is nice of you to ask, but I don't know that I'm ready to actually help at a workshop the way Stephanie does. I don't know enough."

"I don't expect you to be like Stephanie. I would just like you two to come and connect with other teenagers. I'd like to try to draw more teens to my workshops after what I saw here today. If teens come, I will need teen assistants. Just consider it," Mary said. "I am curious about what you have learned from working with your classmates. Why are they drawn to angels do you think?"

"One thing is angels are safe. By that I mean that the Jewish and Muslim kids believe in angels just like Christians do. Even though we are of different faiths, we can agree on something. Several of us were talking about it at lunch, and it was so cool to hear so many different people talk about angels. I don't know exactly what other religions teach, but sitting at the table, it didn't matter. We all believed in God and angels. There was one guy who says he is an atheist, and he really felt left out!" Suzanne said laughing. Angels are something everyone could agree on, and it felt good. Two of the girls who came today are Jewish, and they were cool with coming," said Suzanne.

"Let's go sit by the fountain; I want to hear more," Mary said, and then she led them to chairs by the fountain. "It is lovely here and we can just relax for a few minutes and talk. Anna, why do you think teens are interested in angels?"

"I think it's because they can communicate with them. Most of the kids I know pray whether they go to church or not, but it's hard to know if your prayer has been heard. When I find a penny or see a card that has special meaning, I know I'm being heard. Doesn't everyone need to know they've been heard?" answered Anna as she looked intently into Mary's eyes.

"Yes, I think they do. What about when you don't receive a sign or a card that gives you an answer? What do you do then?" Mary's question was powerful because Anna had only promoted the positive results of communicating with angels.

"I don't know." There had been times when she hadn't received an answer, and a couple girls had complained that they had asked for a sign from their angels and nothing happened. *What had she said to them?* Anna thought. "I suppose my answer is to keep asking and be patient."

"That's the answer I'd give too. Sometimes life just needs to unfold so we can see things. We also can't depend on angels to make all our decisions. That would interfere with the free choice that God gave us."

"Mary, why do you think pastors and youth ministers don't talk about communicating with angels or receiving signs from deceased loved ones? My mom has a book written by hospice nurses that is filled with stories of deceased loved ones sending signs and seeing angels. Wouldn't that be comforting to people who are grieving? I know it helped my mom," Suzanne said as she leaned forward in her chair towards Mary.

"I wish I could answer your question. Maybe you could ask your ministers?"

Both girls laughed out loud. Suzanne said, "My pastor would think I was crazy if I told him I had been communicating with my guardian angels."

Anna agreed, but after considering it for a moment, she added, "Our youth minister is great. I think I'll bring up that book you were talking about, Suzanne, and then go from there. Maybe we could talk about it."

Their conversation was interrupted when Lauren appeared, and they all stood to greet her.

"I didn't want to leave without meeting you. I'm Lauren Adams; I'm married to Anna's father, Dave. I am so fortunate that Anna invited me here today. Under the circumstances it could have been quite uncomfortable, but it turned out to be very nice."

Anna gritted her teeth. *Do you always have to say something that embarrasses me?* She thought.

Mary knew that Karen's ex-husband had remarried, but this was a surprise to meet her in Karen's shop. "I am glad you were able to come. Anna is a wonderful ambassador for angels," Mary said.

"You know she got into this because of a research project. I admit I questioned the validity of her research, since my background is science. However, it turned out very well for her. She showed how skillful she is today when she was able to communicate with that woman's angels," Lauren's said, with forced enthusiasm in her voice.

"Did you receive any helpful information today?" Mary skillfully asked and was able to steer Lauren away from her focus on Anna.

"Well, I received information. I'm not sure how helpful it was," Lauren answered with a scowl. "Stephanie was my partner, and I know she is supposedly good at this, but I just didn't get it."

"What you heard today might have meaning for you later. Stephanie is very good at being able to receive guidance for others, but no one is accurate all the time. Working on receiving your own guidance will probably be the most beneficial. I believe anything one does to become closer to God is beneficial. I know your angels are eager to help you," Mary said reassuringly.

"Thank you. It was truly a pleasure to meet you. Bye, Anna, I'll see you soon," Lauren said, and then she left.

"You can relax now; she's gone," Mary said, looking at Anna.

"What do you mean?" asked Anna innocently.

"Your body language speaks volumes. While she was talking you backed away, and your mouth became a tight line. Working with angels allows people to overcome difficult relationships. I am intuitive in part because I have learned to be a good observer. Believe me. I have worked hard at being patient, tolerant, and loving to difficult people. It has not been easy, but it has been rewarding. That is something you could teach young people," Mary said.

"Only if I can learn how to do it myself," muttered Anna.

Mary laughed. "That is true. But I think you'll be able to. You really are a natural at working with angels, because you have so much faith. Why do you think your faith is so strong?"

"I think it's because I've been raised to believe in a loving God. A loving God would provide guardian angels for his children, and he would have a way that people could communicate with them," Anna said slowly and confidently.

"You have truly been blessed, and you are a blessing to others. There are a lot of teens who could use a dose of your faith in God. I hope you and Suzanne will decide to come to Cincinnati to help. And about Lauren, try asking your angels to help you be more patient and to help you find some good qualities in her."

"I'll think about coming to help, and I will try to overlook Lauren's rude, selfish behavior," Anna said with an ornery grin.

"Maybe not listing her imperfections would be a good place to start," laughed Mary. "Suzanne, it's been a pleasure meeting you, and I hope to see you in Cincinnati. I'll go say good-bye to Karen. Take care of each other."

As Anna and Suzanne helped Karen get the store organized for another business day, Anna thought about her conversation with Mary. What was the main draw for teens, or anybody, to believe they can communicate with angels? She asked herself what had been her most meaningful experience, and it was definitely finding the pennies. She knew without a doubt that God was watching over her when she had picked up that first penny. She had known God was with her when she was mourning her grandmother, and she knew from then on she would find comfort if she asked. Anna found herself humming as she returned the plants that had been moved from the base of the angel fountain. Her favorites were the peace lilies and the gardenias. This was a beautiful spot her mother had created. She hoped people would come in and buy books, sip tea, and maybe discuss angels as they sat by the angel fountain. It would also be nice if they bought some plants too!

Chapter 14

Spring break was quickly approaching, and Anna still had not made her decision about going to Mary's workshop. The workshop was scheduled for the last weekend of spring break. Suzanne wanted to go but not without Anna. Anna was glad that her angel fame had seemed to pass, and she was beginning to feel like a regular person again. She and Thom had gone to dinner and to the Valentine's Day dance with Mark and Maddie. Anna and Thom had spent time with Kevin and Suzanne and other couples too. Thom was a very social guy and loved being surrounded by people. Anna was more reserved, but it had been fun to be in the midst of so many people. Anna felt like she belonged and was accepted. She didn't want to be considered odd or different. Being called Angel Girl had set her apart, and she didn't want that to happen again.

On the other hand, Anna loved her own personal angel work. She still helped classmates who wanted to learn how to use a pendulum or read angel cards. And she worked happily at her mother's store, helping customers and answering their questions about communicating with angels. Perhaps people had just accepted her and her angelic interest. If she started helping Mary, would that bring renewed attention to her? She was very happy with her life now and didn't want to mess it up. Anna knew

Suzanne would be at Maddie's party tonight and would want her answer about going to Cincinnati. She just wished she had the answer. She laughed at herself and thought, *I'm conflicted!*

Anna not only had mixed feelings about helping Mary, she was also had mixed emotions about the night's activities. Mark had planned a surprise party for Maddie's birthday. It was being held at his house, and of course Lauren had gone all out. Anna had suggested roasting hot dogs and making s'mores over a campfire down by the stream, but Lauren had said she thought having the party catered would give the party a touch of elegance. She said she had told Maddie's mother what she had planned and had gotten her full support.

Mark invited almost fifty people. Anna's dad had been amiable about the party, and said he was looking forward to meeting more of Anna's friends. He really was clueless about things. He acted like this was Anna's party too. He didn't realize this was all about Maddie, and of course Lauren.

Suzanne and Kevin were coming together even though Anna knew they hadn't been getting along lately. Kevin was on the football team with Thom, and of course Mark planned to be on the team next fall, so he had invited a lot of football players. Anna thought there were more boys coming than girls, but Maddie would love that too. Anna had not been asked to do anything for the party since her initial suggestion was shot down, so her only concern was a gift for Maddie.

Their friendship had not recovered from the coffee shop conversation; it limped along, and they both seemed to accept the change that had taken place. Double-dating was fun, but that didn't allow time for them to have the girl talk they needed. Being in *My Fair Lady* together had been nice, but since Maddie was Eliza Doolittle, the main character, she hadn't been available to hang out during the rehearsals. Once again Anna was with girls who showed an interest in angels, and she enjoyed being in the chorus and working on sets with them. Maddie was too busy to notice where Anna was or what she was doing. Maddie was indeed the star of the show. Lauren had simply gushed over Maddie before throwing a few complimentary crumbs Anna's way. Anna enjoyed the irony of being a flower shop girl and portraying one on stage. She was happy to be in the cast and had no desire to be the star.

Anna's thoughts were broken by the ringing of the phone. "Oh good, I was hoping to catch you before you left. I wondered if you could come early tonight," Lauren asked.

"I have to work until five; what time do you want me there?"

"Could you be here by six? I want to be sure everything is perfect, and these men are of no help. I need another female to look things over before Maddie gets here. Do you think Maddie suspects?" asked Lauren.

"No, I don't. She was flattered that you have a gift for her, and she keeps asking me if I know what it is. Mark told her they needed to stop by before he took her to dinner, because you and Dave were going out tonight. She'll be totally surprised," Anna said reassuringly.

"Oh, I hope you're right. I want this be the best party she has ever had! Can you be here at six then?"

"Yes, I'll have Thom meet me there. I need to get to work now, so I'll see you tonight," Anna said as she clicked off the phone. *Maddie, the wonderful, talented, perfect Maddie!* She thought sarcastically. *I hope my dad still realizes who the daughter in the family is, and it's not Maddie!*

Anna arrived right at six and had to admit the house looked incredible. A bouquet of pastel balloons shaped liked spring flowers greeted the guests in the foyer. Lauren had put pots of daffodils and tulips in strategic places so the feeling of spring carried throughout the house. It had been a warm March day, and the windows were opened with the fresh smell of spring in the rooms. The caterers were busy arranging the table in the dining room, and Lauren was in the kitchen talking to Mark and Dave. Anna followed the sound of Lauren's voice.

"Where should we put the presents? Do you think the hearth in the family room is okay? I didn't think to arrange a table for them," Lauren said in a worried voice.

"Anna, you're just in time," Mark said smiling as she entered the room. "Mom is freaking out over where to put the presents."

"I am not freaking out! I just forgot to plan for a present table."

"I think the hearth is a good place for the presents. I'll start with mine," Anna said as she turned toward the family room. When she entered, she noticed Lauren had placed a picture on the mantel. It was a picture of Maddie and Mark taken at the Valentine's Day dance. She was staring at it when her father came up behind her.

"Lauren had to put that out for the party. I don't like photographs on the mantel; I like pieces of art, but Lauren said it would only be for the party and then it goes back in the living room," Anna's father explained, and he moved a carved wooden bird a little closer to the photograph.

"I didn't think you liked to display photographs anywhere," Anna said without turning to look at her dad.

"Sure, I do. Just not on the mantel. Lauren has photographs all over the place. Haven't you noticed?" asked Dave, surprised by her comment.

Anna turned and looked at her father as she spoke. "Yes, Dad, I've noticed. I've also noticed that the photographs I've given you never seem to make it to a wall or a table. Do you keep them in a box or something?"

"What are talking about? We have pictures of you all over the house," Anna's dad said, clearly irritated.

"No, you have pictures of you, Lauren, and Mark. Now you have a picture of Maddie," Anna said evenly.

"This is crazy!" her dad's voice boomed. "Come!"

Anna followed her father into the living room where there were several photographs on the wall. None, of course, included Anna. She then followed him into his study. The wall was covered with photographs. None were of Anna.

Anna's father was completely surprised to find out Anna was not included in any of the family pictures. He simply had not paid attention. He walked to his desk and picked up Anna's picture in a silver frame. It was taken when she was seven. She was smiling and her two front teeth were missing. She had a butterfly painted on her cheek, and her father's arms were around her. His face was right next to hers and there was no mistaking she was his daughter.

"I have this picture of the two of us. It has always been on my desk. You know that. I look at it every day. I'm sorry I haven't kept up. I should have. I assumed your pictures were included with the rest of ours," he said, realizing Anna was right.

"It's okay, Dad. I know decorating isn't your thing," Anna said, wishing she hadn't brought it up. *I should have kept my mouth shut. But I would like to know where all the pictures I've given dad over the years are,* she thought. She did feel better after seeing her picture sitting on her dad's desk. It made her think she still was Daddy's girl.

"I wondered where you two had gone," Lauren said as she stood in the doorway to the study. "Mark has left to pick up Maddie. People should be arriving soon. What are you two doing in here?"

"We were looking for pictures of Anna. She appears to have been overlooked when it came to displaying photographs." Anna had never heard her father use that tone with Lauren before.

"Really? That can't be right. I'm sure I included her," Lauren said defensively.

"No, Lauren, you didn't," Dave said firmly.

"Well, I can't do anything about it now. We have guests coming and the caterer needs to talk to me. I need you two available to answer the door and show people where to go. Pictures of Anna are not a priority right now," Lauren said in a huff and left.

"They will be later, Lauren. I guarantee they will be," Dave muttered, and he turned to Anna. "I'm sorry. I want this to be your home too. I'm so glad we are in the same town again, and I want you to feel at home here. I'll do better by paying closer attention to a lot of things that are going on. I love you, honey, and I will not allow you to be overlooked."

"I love you too, Dad," said Anna as she gave him a hug. "Come on, we have a party to help with!" Anna really wanted the picture conversation to end. It was easier to talk about the party, but it sure felt good to hear her dad come to her defense.

The brief discussion between Anna's father and Lauren was the first crack in the perfectly planned evening. Things were definitely amiss. The elegant affair that Lauren had planned was a little too elegant for football players. The boys acted like they were afraid they'd break something, and the girls were acting like debutants on display. It was as if everyone was trying to act grown-up instead of just enjoying the birthday party. Maddie was the exception. She thrived on being the birthday girl. She laughed and talked and ... flirted.

Kevin, Suzanne's boyfriend, was the focus of Maddie's attention. Mark had made the mistake of talking to Suzanne, and that set Maddie off. She was the arrow and Kevin was the target. Unfortunately for Suzanne, Maddie had hit the bulls-eye with Kevin. He was enamored by her, and she sparkled in his personal spotlight.

Mark retaliated by spending more time with Suzanne, and by the end of the evening, both couples had developed a relationship virus. The virus was quick to infect, and its result was deadly.

Anna's father hovered close to Anna most of the evening in his attempt to show his interest in her and her friends. This made Thom spend more time with the guys than Anna, and her dad learned way too much about what was going on in her life; primarily, the angel workshop in Cincinnati.

"I didn't realize that your enthusiasm for angels had risen to the level of working with Mary Matson. I hope she is not using you and Suzanne because you're young and naïve," Anna's dad said after listening to Suzanne talk about the upcoming workshop. "If you do decide to go, I don't want you two driving to Cincinnati by yourselves. You are only seventeen years old. Your mother better be planning on taking you."

"Dad, can we talk about this later? This is a party, remember? I think we should have Maddie open her presents because people are starting to leave." Anna left to find Maddie.

"Maddie, how about opening your presents while people eat your birthday cake?" Anna suggested. Maddie agreed and Anna took charge, urging people to get a piece of cake and then go into the family room.

"This is so nice. I can't believe all of you came, and there are so many gifts! This is really too much," Maddie said as she sat down by the stone hearth.

People talked and laughed and seemed to settle into a party mood as they ate rich chocolate fudge cake and listened to Maddie read her birthday cards. Mark had told people they didn't need to bring a gift, but the girls all brought gifts because that's what girls do, even if the invitation says not to. Anna had created a scrapbook of pictures from *My Fair Lady*, which Maddie gushed over. Suzanne gave Maddie a gift certificate to the coffee shop, and all the other girls gave Maddie something to do with angels. She opened three decks of angel cards, angel stationary, angel jewelry, and two angel figurines. Maddie had never made it known that she didn't share Anna's interest in angels, so the girls all assumed that since she was Anna's best friend, she too was into angels. Obviously, it was a wrong assumption.

Maddie was a gracious gift receiver as she opened one angel gift after another, but the tight mouth and drawn brows showed how she really felt.

"Thank you all for making my birthday so special. I think I have enough angel items to open my own angel boutique," she said with a weak laugh. "Anna, your mom is going to have to restock her shelves." She looked at Anna and shook her head as if to say, *I can't believe I received all this angel stuff when you know how I feel.*

The guests broke up into small groups and some left. The party was waning, but the entertainment was just beginning. Lauren asked Maddie to come into the kitchen so she could give her gift privately. It was a beautiful silver necklace with a half carat diamond in a starburst setting.

"This is the most beautiful necklace I have ever seen!" Maddie exclaimed as she hugged Lauren. "Thank you so much!"

"I've always wanted a daughter, and now I feel like I have one. You are like a shining star, so this necklace had to be yours. I am so glad Mark found you and brought you into our family," Lauren said lovingly.

Anna and her father had entered during the gift unveiling and were both struck by Lauren's words. Anna turned and left, but her father stayed and waited for Maddie to leave with her precious gift. They kept their voices low, but it was clear an argument was in progress. Dave's eyes had been opened tonight, and their marriage was going to feel the impact of him no longer being blind.

Anna went to find Thom. She needed to feel his arms around her, and then she wanted to get out of there. The daffodils said it was spring, but it felt like Halloween in the witch's castle.

When Maddie went to show Mark her necklace, she found him talking to Suzanne. She confidently displayed Lauren's stamp of approval and told Suzanne to move along to someone else's boyfriend. Mark told Maddie he had had enough of her queenly ways and left the room. Kevin walked forward to comfort the crying Maddie, and Anna just stared. After Kevin comforted Maddie, she headed for Anna, holding her necklace in her hand. Maddie's tears had stopped, and she apparently wanted Anna's support.

"I can't believe Lauren gave me such an expensive gift. I'm going to have to make up with Mark just to keep Lauren happy. She would be devastated if we broke up after giving me this necklace." Maddie paused while she put the necklace on and Anna watched. "How does it look? Is the chain the right length, do you think?"

"It's perfect, Maddie," Anna said, aching inside, and she squeezed Thom's hand. She looked at Thom and mentally communicated, *We need to leave now!* But Maddie continued her all-about-me chatter. "Lauren is amazing. She thinks of me as her daughter. I knew she liked me, but I didn't know she did to this extent! Are you okay? You look a little pale. Maybe you should get something to drink. I need to go find Mark and apologize for whatever he thinks I did." With that said, Maddie left and Anna pulled Thom to the door.

Thom tried to talk on the drive to Anna's house, but she wasn't ready to talk. Her mother and Dan were out for the evening, so Thom and Anna had the house to themselves.

"That was quite a party," Thom said as they sat down on the couch in Anna's family room, and he put his arm around her.

"I'll say. I don't think it could have been worse," Anna said glumly.

"Sure it could have. No one threw any punches or broke anything," Thom said, trying to lighten the mood.

"Apparently you're not counting the broken hearts," Anna said softly.

"I'm sorry. Yours is one of them. Lauren is a jerk. You are the one she should have given that necklace to, not Maddie. Lauren just fell under Maddie's spell like many of us have." Anna looked at him, waiting. "You know I was under it for a couple of years," Thom said, reflecting back on the time he spent in awe of Maddie.

"I don't care about the stupid necklace. It was the total lack of acknowledging she has a daughter. I am only a stepdaughter, but I have been one for three years. To hear her say that, and to see Maddie's picture on the mantle, was just too much to take. There are no pictures of me in the house except on Daddy's desk." Anna realized she had just referred to her father as "Daddy." Thom pulled her closer, and she cried while he stroked her hair and patted her comfortingly.

"My guess is Mark will break up with Maddie. After the way she threw herself at Kevin in front of everybody, I can't imagine he'll stay with her," Thom said, "He must be attracted to the self-absorbed type of girl because he said his last girlfriend was like that."

"I doubt if Suzanne is too heartbroken over Kevin, because they have been arguing a lot lately. But it still had to hurt to see him completely succumb to Maddie's spell." Anna ached for Suzanne. "Nobody at the party could have missed the way Kevin completely ignored Suzanne and was totally captivated by Maddie. Suzanne probably wanted to leave before we did."

Anna felt comforted nestled under Thom's arm. They sat quietly, and Anna thought about the night's events. She never thought her father would stand up against Lauren. She had to admit she was proud of her dad and was beginning to believe that Lauren hadn't completely taken him away from her. Anna always knew that Lauren didn't like her; but like it or not, she was her stepdaughter. *Sorry, Lauren, you're stuck with me, and I'm stuck with you,* she told herself. *As for Maddie, well, our friendship will never be like it was. I need to accept the fact that we've changed and move on. Mark must feel awful. He is crazy about Maddie, and he planned a great birthday for her. She is such a princess!* Anna's thoughts were interrupted by Thom gently kissing her.

"Are you okay? Can I do anything? You look so sad," Thom said.

"I am sad, but I'll be better tomorrow. Just keep on holding me for a while. You're what I need right now," Anna said as she cuddled even closer to Thom.

"With pleasure, my lady," Thom said before kissing her. Thom's sweet kisses erased the evening's ugly events, and her troubles were temporarily forgotten as Thom soothed her troubled heart. Love did heal all wounds.

Chapter 15

Anna spent most of Sunday in her grandmother's room reading. She wanted to forget the events of Maddie's birthday party. She loved her grandmother's journals and her book collection. She had called Suzanne and only briefly talked about Kevin. Suzanne said he had taken her home from the party, and when she got out of the car, she told him it was over. That was that, and she didn't want to discuss Kevin because she was tired of crying. She was determined to move forward, and she wanted to talk about going to the angel workshop. Anna said she still hadn't decided, but she would decide today.

"Why is this such a big decision for you? I don't get it. I thought you loved talking about angels," Suzanne asked, more than a little frustrated with Anna.

"I do like talking about angels, and I would like to learn more at Mary's workshop, I just don't want to be responsible for teaching others, and I don't want people to look at me like I'm weird. Why can't we go and be students like everyone else?"

"Maybe we can. Mary hasn't told us what she wants us to do. Let's go, and when we get there, we'll talk to her. She might not want us to do anything but be with the other teens. Why would anyone look at you like you're weird? They're at the workshop too! You haven't gotten over that newspaper article Amber wrote, have you?"

"Amber's editorial made everyone at school know me as the Angel Girl, and it took a while to be called Anna. I am once again Anna, and I like that. Mary's a famous author. What if she wants to use our names as teen helpers? I don't want to go back to being called Angel Girl." Anna explained her fears honestly and hoped Suzanne was listening.

"I hear what you are saying, but I can think of a lot worse things to be called than Angel Girl. Think about it and call me later. We do need to let Mary know if we are coming or not."

"I promise I'll call you tonight."

Karen was at the shop, but someone else was closing, so her mother would be home early. Anna hung up the phone and picked up one of her grandmother's journals and began reading. "What seems the most challenging task frequently gives the biggest rewards," Anna read. "Introduce your friends to their angels, and they will meet God. The amount of strength someone has is equal to their amount of faith." Sentence after sentence leapt from the pages as if someone was personally selecting them for Anna to read. She was still reading when her mom walked in.

"It looks like you've been busy," Karen said as she saw all the books on the floor. "Did you find what you were looking for?"

"I think so. I've been trying to decide about going to Mary's workshop. Suzanne really wants to go and help, but I'm not so sure about the helping part. Grandma's journals seem to be telling me I should go and stop being a wuz!"

"Ask your angels for help! They help wuzzes all the time!" Karen said as she hugged her daughter and looked at all of her mother's books and journals on the floor, "So does this mean you're going?"

"I think I will. It'll be fun, right?"

"Absolutely. You and Suzanne will have fun together, and Mary will be thrilled you two are coming."

"I hope she doesn't have high hopes of what we can do, but I am curious to see what a whole workshop is like," said Anna as she finished putting her grandmother's books back on the shelves."

"I don't think you'll be sorry you decided to go." Anna's mom hesitated while she straightened the books. "I've been meaning to tell you that I saw Lauren at the grocery the other day. She was complimentary of my shop. She really isn't the wicked witch you make her out to be."

"I have had such a nice afternoon, do we really have to talk about Lauren?"

"Yes, we do. Somehow you've got to accept her as your dad's wife. She loves your dad, and he loves her. I'd like you to try and think of things you like about her and focus on that. Now, I know you can name one thing."

"All right, she makes Dad happy. But I don't know why. She is so—" Anna was interrupted by her mother.

"You can't throw in anything negative while you are saying positive things," Karen warned.

"Okay, fine. She has a flair for decorating, and she knows how to cook. Is that enough?" asked Anna, showing her frustration.

"What about some inner qualities? Does she have any strengths that you admire?"

Anna had to think about this one. "I admire that she worked hard to become a pharmacist. Does that count?"

"Yes. Anything else?"

"I like how she is with Mark. She is supportive and loving. She's like that with Dad too." *I am the outsider. Lauren wants it that way.* Anna's thoughts were revealed on her face.

"I see that look on your face; whatever you're thinking stop," Karen said firmly. "You must try to control your thoughts. Every time you think of something you don't like about her, you make it harder to accept her. Picture a time you saw Lauren making Mark or your dad happy." She watched Anna's face. "Okay, now put that picture in your memory bank. Lauren gives love and happiness to two people you care about, and that gives you something in common. I might add that she has shown an interest in angels, which is another commonality."

"I'd rather she'd stayed away from the angel workshop, but I admit there have been a few occasions when she hasn't been too hateful," Anna said begrudgingly.

"Well, that's progress. Focus on those times. Send Lauren love and ask for understanding and patience. You can't change her. You can only change your thoughts and feelings. Pray for help in loving someone who is difficult. Remember, Jesus taught that it is easy to love people who are loving, but God's challenge is to love those who are not."

"I know; Grandma used to say that all the time when I would complain about someone." Anna paused and continued. "Dad called today. He said he wanted me to know that his home was my home and there were going to be some changes. He asked me to forgive him for not paying better attention to my feelings. He said he and Lauren had a long talk and she wants to develop a relationship with me, but she has never felt I'd let her. See? She has to blame me!"

"Give her a chance to try. I'm glad your father is rooting for you now. Lauren isn't all bad. She'll eventually learn that your dad is capable of loving you and her. You need to work on you being more accepting of Lauren." Karen stood up and said, "I think this is a Lorenzo's night. You have twenty minutes to get ready. Italian food cures all woes!"

Before going to bed that night, Anna called Suzanne and then emailed Mary and told her she and Suzanne would both be there next Friday for the opening session. Since it would be spring break, they would have no problem getting there early on Friday so that Mary could prepare them for the weekend activities. The workshop was scheduled to begin Friday night and end at noon on Sunday. Suzanne's mom said she would take the girls and stay for the workshop, since all the adults agreed that the girls were not driving to Cincinnati by themselves.

Late Thursday evening, the night before the angel workshop, Suzanne called. Her brother was in the hospital having an emergency appendectomy and both parents were with him. There was no way her mother could take them to Cincinnati the next day. Anna knew her mother couldn't leave the store on such short notice, but maybe her dad could drive them down and her mother could pick them up on Sunday. She called and Lauren answered. She hadn't talked to Lauren since the party and didn't really want to.

"May I speak to my dad, please?" Anna said politely.

"I'll get him," Lauren replied, equally polite.

"Hey, Anna, how are you?" Her dad cheerfully greeted her.

"I have a problem, and I'm hoping you can help,"

"Sure, if I can."

Anna explained about needing someone to take them to Cincinnati.

"I figured you'd decide to help Ms. Matson with her angel business. If that's what you want, then I'm not going to stand in your way. But I have a meeting with a client tomorrow morning, so I can't take you, honey. I'm sorry. I could pick you up on Sunday if you can find someone to get you there."

"Okay, Dad, I'll let you know. Thanks." Anna hung up unhappily. There had to be someone who could take them. As she was thinking, the phone rang.

"Hello?"

"Anna, it's Lauren. Your dad just told me you need someone to drive you to Cincinnati. Tomorrow is my day off, and I'd be glad to take you and Suzanne, if you'd let me."

Anna didn't know what to say. They had to leave the next morning and it was ten o'clock at night. She didn't have time to be choosey. Mark had told Anna that he had come down pretty hard on his mom for the crazy way she acted about Maddie. He also said that he had ended it with Maddie the day after the party, and Lauren was blaming herself for the breakup. Apparently Lauren thought that doing so much for Maddie had scared her away. The nice news was that Mark actually told Lauren that he thought she had hurt Anna's feelings. Realizing that both her Dad and Mark had come to her defense made it easier to be nice to Lauren.

"That would be great, Lauren. Thanks. We'd like to leave about nine tomorrow morning, if that would work for you," Anna said uncertainly.

"That'll be fine. I'll be at your house at nine."

The drive to Cincinnati was fairly uneventful. There was no mention of Maddie or the party. The conversation centered on angels, and Suzanne happily chatted about what she had read and what she thought they might be doing at the workshop.

"Would you give a message to Mary's assistant Stephanie for me?" Lauren asked Anna while keeping her eyes on the road.

"Sure."

"Tell her she was right,"

Anna would have loved to ask what Stephanie had been right about, but of course she couldn't, so she just said, "I'll tell her."

"Thanks, I'd appreciate it."

Suzanne picked up the conversation by suggesting ways she and Anna could reach teens. "A website is a must. We could answer questions and ask kids to tell us how working with angels helps them. I think there would be a lot of interest in it."

As they got closer to Cincinnati, Anna was noticeably getting nervous.

"I just hope I'm qualified to do this. I don't want to let Mary down," Anna said, expressing her fears. "I've been praying for a sign that this is what I should do, but I haven't received one, so maybe this isn't what I need to do."

"Maybe you received one and didn't recognize it," suggested Suzanne.

"No, I'd recognize it," Anna said confidently.

"We're almost there. The hotel is on the next block. Dave will be here Sunday at 2:00 p.m. like you asked. Just call if there is a change in the time. I know this will be an awesome experience for you both. And, Anna, you'll be just fine," Lauren said sincerely.

"Thanks, Lauren. It was really nice of you to drive us here. We probably wouldn't have made it if you hadn't." *Lauren was nice to me! She might not hate me after all. Come on, angels, help me give Lauren a chance.*

"I'm glad I could do something to help," said Lauren, and it was clear she really meant it.

I'm going to have to recast Lauren as my fairy godmother if she keeps this up. She isn't fitting the part of a wicked witch now.

Lauren parked in front of the hotel, and the girls gathered their things from the trunk. As Anna stepped into the hotel lobby, something caught her eye. A penny winked at her from the red carpeting. As she reached to pick up her sign, she thanked her angels. *I can do this; I can do this; I can do this,* she told herself repeatedly.

Mary and Stephanie both greeted the girls warmly. "I am so glad you are here. We have 110 people registered for this weekend, and twenty of them are teenagers. Stephanie will go over the

schedule with you and show you the room we'll be working in."
Mary's excitement was contagious. Anna was eager to hear what
was expected of her and Suzanne. "I will introduce you girls
tonight. All I ask is that you watch the teens and see their reactions
to what I am saying, and listen for their questions. When we get
into groups, join a group with a couple teenagers in it. We will see
what happens tonight and go from there. I really want to make
this meaningful for the young people who are here, and I think
you two are the ones who can make that happen." Mary hugged
both girls and left them in Stephanie's care.

Anna was relieved to hear what Mary expected. *This won't be
hard at all*, she thought.

"Tonight will be fun. Most people don't know what to expect
and are a little apprehensive," Stephanie explained. "Mary will
give an overview of this weekend's schedule. She'll teach a
meditation and talk about the importance of quieting one's mind
before praying. We'll practice breathing and ridding our minds
of distractions. She'll talk about seeing colors in the mind's eye.
People will be asked to get into groups of five or six and share
what brought them here this weekend. You will really enjoy
hearing this. Do you have any questions?" Stephanie asked. The
girls didn't, so Stephanie told them to enjoy themselves for the
next few hours.

Anna said, "Let's get something to eat and see what stores are
around here. Maybe we can find something new to wear tonight."
The air was cool and smelled fresh and clean. There were several
small shops to explore, and the afternoon passed quickly.

The girls were early for the opening session of the workshop.
They wanted to find the teenagers who had registered. The room
was filled with nervous anticipation as the girls stood up front
watching the seats being taken. Women clearly outnumbered

the men, and there was a noticeable range of ages in the participants.

Mary began right on time and welcomed everyone. She introduced Stephanie and another adult helper, Torie. Anna and Suzanne had met Torie when they returned from their shopping. She was tall with straight, black hair. Her eyes were light blue. She had a calmness about her that seemed to affect those around her. She was in her mid-forties, but there was something about her that seemed ageless.

Mary then introduced Anna and Suzanne as her teen assistants. Anna's stomach began to churn, aware of all the curious eyes examining her and Suzanne. She was glad that Mary quickly moved on to leading the group in a meditation.

Anna loved the meditation, and her head filled with shades of purple and blue. She knew she had cleared her mind of worry and was ready to hear angelic guidance. Suzanne headed for one group and Anna another when the large group divided into smaller groups.

Anna was drawn to a group where a girl who would be characterized as goth or emo was seated. Anna felt the girl's eyes on her as she joined the circle. Each person in the group drew a card with a number. The cards were numbered one to six. Mary's idea was to try to provide structure for the small groups so that everyone would have an opportunity to share. Anyone holding number three was asked to introduce herself and tell why she had come for the weekend, or what she was most interested in learning about.

A woman in her forties held number three. "My name is Nicole Lester, and I came because I have read a number of books on communicating with angels and the deceased. I am pretty sure I have received messages, but I would like to hear what others have experienced." There was still time before Mary read the next number, and the group sat uncomfortably wondering what to do.

Anna spoke hesitantly. "I have received signs from my guardian angels. They have left me pennies. Has anyone else received signs?"

A woman who looked to be in her fifties spoke. "I'm Lois, and I have had several experiences that I'm sure most people would say were coincidences. I admit, at first I thought they were, but I don't anymore. I believe, without a doubt, that I have angels watching over me. I find it comforting."

The goth girl asked, "What do you mean by comforting?"

"Well, at my age, life has tossed me around a bit. There were times I wasn't so sure I could make it. I know there are more difficulties to face before I pass, and I am thankful I won't have to handle them alone," Lois said as she looked into the faces of the young women in the group.

Lois was interrupted by Mary calling the next number.

"I'm number two," said a young woman in her mid-twenties. "My name is Marie, and I came because my mother has terminal cancer, and I am having trouble dealing with it. I need to believe she will still be with me after she dies. I am hoping that I will learn something to convince me I won't lose her completely. I thought there might be people here who would talk about their experiences with deceased loved ones."

"I'm sorry about your mom. My grandmother died of cancer last fall, and she has visited me. Once I heard her voice, and another time I smelled her perfume, so I know it happens," Anna added softly.

The group gave Marie encouragement about being able to receive messages from the other side and showed great understanding for what she was going through. Number one was called, and the goth girl spoke.

"My name is Amber, and I came to get my mother off my back. I was getting into Wicca, and she freaked out about it. Once she read one of my books, she chilled, but she said if all these spells required prayer, I should be directing my prayers in the right direction. That means toward her God. She found an angel book written by a Wiccan, so I read it. I agreed to come today because my mother believes in angels, and I'm not against the idea of having angels hanging around me."

"I may know the book you are talking about, or one like it," said Anna.

"Really?" asked Amber with a mixture of surprise and doubt.

"I didn't read all of it, but I did a research paper on angels; one of the books I used was written by a Wiccan, but I don't remember her name. It was white with a cool angel on the front, with her arms uplifted. The author wrote about using a pendulum and cards. Does any of that sound the same?" asked Anna.

"Yes."

"Did you read about making an angel rosary to use in prayer?" asked Anna.

"I made one," Amber said.

"No way; I'd love to see it," Anna said enthusiastically.

Amber visibly relaxed once Anna had started talking to her. It was obvious that she was used to being treated as an object of curiosity. The purple streaks in her jet black hair and her heavy black eyeliner drew attention to her. She had a pretty face, but it was covered with such a light make-up base that she looked like a ghost. Her black shirt, black jeans with silver studs, and black boots all contributed to a goth look.

They weren't able to talk anymore because number four was announced. A woman in her thirties spoke. "I'm Sara, and I came because I need support in holding my marriage together. We've been married ten years and have two children. We decided that I would stay home with the kids, and he would bring home the paychecks. Things aren't going very well right now; in fact, it's awful. I need help."

Lois spoke. "I can feel your unhappiness, and I am curious what you expect to happen this weekend to help you."

"I want someone who can hear my angels to tell me what to do," Sara said.

"I don't think it works that way. I think angels support us, but they can't make our decisions for us. That's the responsibility of each individual. God gave us free will, which means we are free to make our own decisions. Would you really want someone to tell you to leave your husband, or get a job outside your home, or ... I don't know ... anything important like that?" Lois asked patiently, like a caring mother.

"Yes," Sara admitted in a meek voice.

"Well, honey, I don't think it's going to happen. Many people like someone else to make their decisions for them so they don't have to take responsibility for the outcomes. Perhaps you'll discover this weekend that you are strong enough to make your own decision. God and his angels give us strength and insight into our problems if we ask. I know they have helped me."

A discussion ensued and ended when number six was called. "You already know I am Lois, and I came because I wanted to hear other people's stories, and I want to learn how to do angel readings. I have a deck of angel cards, but I visited a woman who didn't use cards. She was able to tell me a lot about my situation by holding my hands. She wasn't a psychic; she called herself an angel intuitive. I have visited psychics over the years and have had some good and bad readings. This angel lady was the best I have ever gone to. I thought maybe I could learn how to do what she did."

Anna's was the last number to be called. "I'm here to help Mary. I am the third generation of angel believers. Mary asked my friend and me to show other teenagers how they can meet their angels and receive their heavenly support. I am a beginner and here to learn like the rest of you, and I admit I'm nervous about this weekend."

When the evening came to a close, the small group had developed a sense of family. They shared a desire of learning more, and they had demonstrated genuine concern for each other's situations. Their angels had to be smiling at the willingness each member had shown in reaching out to someone else in the group. As for Anna, she felt inadequate to help others because her experiences were so few compared to Lois's. She had so much to learn, but she was willing to try.

Chapter 16

Saturday's session began with a different feeling. Since people had been in small groups the night before, they had met others, and a comfort level had been established. Many were greeting each other and sitting with newfound friends. Mary began by asking people to fill out cards with questions they would like answered. She then led the group through a meditation. Once again the participants were going to be divided into groups. Today's groups would be divided by age.

Teenagers were asked to get into groups of six, as were people in their twenties, thirties, forties, fifties, and sixties. Mary asked them to spend a few minutes getting acquainted and then select a partner. Amber and Anna chose the same group, and they became partners. Suzanne was in another group with a girl, Lily, she had met the night before.

Lily and Suzanne were partners for the first activity. Each couple was asked to join hands, close their eyes, and try to feel something about the other person. They were to notice any colors that filled their heads and ask the other person's angels for any messages. Suzanne held Lily's thin hands, and a feeling of sickness filled Suzanne. She followed Mary's directive and asked Lily's angels for any messages. All she saw in her mind's eye was green, waves and waves of green. She knew that green meant healing.

When it was time to share, Suzanne told Lily what she had seen, and Lily began to cry. She said she had come this weekend to please her mother. Friends at school had gone to the school nurse about her not eating. Everyone seemed to think she was anorexic. Her mother was making her go to counseling, and Lily was furious with her mother. She agreed to come this weekend with hopes of getting out of counseling. She said last night someone in her group told her she would pray for her to get well.

"They assumed I have some terrible illness like cancer. Maybe I do need help," Lily said.

"I believe if you pray for help, you'll receive it. I know you have angels with you always. Look at them as friends who can help you with this problem. I know you don't want to go to counseling, but maybe you could use something you learn this weekend to help you. Perhaps you need the courage to go to counseling. Lots of people go to counseling for lots of different reasons. 'Sometimes the things we are most afraid to try are the things we need most.' That's a quote from my mom," Suzanne said with a little laugh. "Were you able to receive anything about me?"

"I felt warmth and a sense of peace. I didn't hear anything, but I just felt like you were a caring person. Maybe your angels were letting me know what a good person you are," Lily said.

"Thanks. I'm trying." Suzanne didn't know what to say, so she just kept looking at Lily, waiting for more.

"As pretty as you are, I bet a lot of girls give you a hard time," Lily said, looking at Suzanne's dark blue eyes, flawless skin, and finely chiseled nose. Her dark brown hair was thick and cut in a style that emphasized her eyes.

Suzanne's first reaction was to say Lily was wrong, but instead she thought about what Lily had said. "I never really thought about my looks making people dislike me, but girls sometimes assume I am stuck-up because I apparently look very preppy. They don't even try to get to know me."

"The girls who do get to know you see how kind you are," Lily said sweetly.

"Thank you. I am lucky to have made some good friends, but it wasn't until I got interested in angels that I started meeting girls outside of my group. I'm sure some kids thought I was stuck-up. I guess my interest in angels made me see others differently, and hopefully others saw me differently too. Angels are what brought Anna and me together."

Participants were asked to find a new partner within their group, and once again, they asked their partner's angels for any messages. Many participants were successful in receiving some information about their partners, so the room was filled with a sense of accomplishment and spiritual awakening. People shared within their groups, and Mary, Stephanie, and Torie visited as many groups as they could. There were tears, laughter, and appreciation expressed in response to messages received. Most were humbled knowing that they had been the conduit between an angel or a deceased loved one and their partner.

Amber and Lily both joined Anna and Suzanne for lunch. A giant salad bar with warm rolls was provided as part of the workshop in the hotel. With the exception of Lily, the girls piled their plates high. Lily took a few pieces of fruit and spread them out on the plate so it would look full; she added a roll, no butter.

"I've never understood chicks who don't eat. Are you a model or something?" Amber asked Lily about halfway through lunch.

Lily stared at Amber and then answered, "No, I'm not a model. I eat enough. I'm just a picky eater."

Suzanne gave Amber a look that said, *Back off.*

"Hey, I'm sorry. It's none of my business whether you eat or not. I just can't imagine not enjoying food. You can see from my body that I don't miss a meal," Amber said good-naturedly.

"It's okay. Lots of people are on my case about not eating. I do eat; if I eat too much I get sick. Then I get yelled at for throwing up. I apparently have issues with food," Lily said, and tears filled her eyes.

"Are you anorexic or something?" asked Amber.

"Or something," replied Lily.

"Lily is here to see if meeting her angels could help her. Isn't that right, Lily?" asked Suzanne, gently prodding Lily to share.

"Yes. It is a deal I made with my mother. She's pushing counseling because she got a call from my school, so I thought if I came here I could get out of counseling," Lily explained to Anna and Amber.

"Counseling isn't so bad. If you have the right counselor it can be helpful." Amber hesitated and then continued. "At least, it was for me."

"You went to counseling?" Lily asked in her soft voice.

"Yeah, for almost a year. And it helped me resolve some issues. My mother still thinks I have more to work on, but the counseling is now on an as-needed basis. Give it a try. It really isn't so bad," Amber said, trying to be encouraging.

"I need to make it through this weekend first, and then I'll think about the counseling." Lily had her head down as she spoke.

"Well, this morning was fun, wasn't it? Nothing scary, and you felt good about it, right?" asked Suzanne cheerily. "I think this afternoon will be even better. How did it go for you two this morning?" Suzanne asked Amber and Anna, trying to get the attention off of Lily.

"I had a good morning. I am always surprised when I say something to my partner that is correct and helpful. It just doesn't make sense that I receive information about total strangers and they understand it," said Anna, shaking her head and buttering a roll.

"I had a good morning too, and my mom was thrilled with what she was told by someone in her group," said Amber smiling. "She also must be jumping for joy because I'm with some 'preps' for a change. She thinks my friends have heavy, dark energy and it isn't good for me. She's really into this energy stuff. I have to admit you are a surprise, Anna."

"Why is that?" asked Anna.

"You go to church and you are into this metaphysical stuff. I didn't think the two went together."

"You have to add Suzanne to the list of churchgoers. I'm into angels. I don't know about other metaphysical things. Well, I do know deceased loved ones visit us, so I guess that would be considered metaphysical. I like going to church, and there are angels in the church, so it fits. My pastor talks about God's love, and that's what angels are for me, a sign of his love. I do learn things in church that help me, and I like the time to pray and meditate. You should try it," Anna suggested to Amber.

Amber laughed. "I used to go. It's not for me. It's for my mom."

"I want to talk more about your mother's comment about people's energies," said Suzanne. "Have you noticed the energies of the people who are here?" Suzanne asked Amber.

"Yeah, most people have a lightness about them. I can feel positive energy coming from them. I guess I relaxed when I realized that Anna knew something about Wiccans." She looked at Anna. "I had you pegged as a snobby prep, but you turned out to be pretty decent," Amber said with a smile. "I had to drop my heavy doubting energy in order to give this stuff a try. So far, I have been impressed with what I've seen and been able to do."

"I liked having you as my partner. We were great together. I like how direct and honest you are about everything."

"Thanks. Since I am honest," Amber said with an ornery grin, "there are some people here that are just plain weird."

Lily surprised everyone by saying, "I agree with Amber. One woman is so deep into this stuff I couldn't even understand her. She wanted to clean my chakras and have her friend do Reiki on me. I don't even know what that is!" she said with a light laugh, and the girls joined her in laughing.

"In spite of some of the strangeness, I like learning all these things. There are some amazing people here. Mary said that tonight some women have agreed to teach classes in their area of expertise. She's going to announce it after lunch," Anna said.

The girls finished lunch and talked about some of the other teens they had met. One girl, Mina, said she had been talking to her guardian angels since she was a toddler. Her parents called them her imaginary friends until her mother realized they were the girl's angels. Mina said that one day when she was three, she told her mother not come in her room until her friends stopped singing. When her mother did enter Mina's room, she was swaying to some silent music and saying bye to the ceiling. Mina's mom asked what her friends looked like, and Mina said, sparkles. That was it. From then on, her mother talked to Mina about her angel friends.

Another girl said she had angel friends when she was little too, but her family punished her for talking to them. Her mother told her she didn't want people to think she had a crazy daughter who talked to an invisible person. When asked how she knew it was her guardian angel, the girl said she just knew. Coming to this workshop was important to her because she wanted to meet others who believed in angels, and she was hoping to reconnect with hers.

Lunch ended on a happy note, and the girls were ready for whatever the afternoon session would bring. Mary began by announcing that individuals from the group would conduct mini sessions that night from 7:00 p.m. to 8:30 p.m. The topics were reincarnation, divining tools such as pendulums and cards, chakras, auras, Reiki, crystals, and ghosts. There would be sign-up sheets at the end of the afternoon.

The afternoon session began with Mary discussing angels in various religions and human encounters with them. She then moved on to deceased loved ones. People were asked to get into mixed groups. The goal was to have as many different ages represented as possible. As in the morning session, the small groups spent time introducing themselves before choosing a partner. Each partner took turns asking to receive information from their partner's deceased loved ones. People throughout the room were rewarded with messages from loved ones.

Total strangers knowing a grandmother's nickname, a name of a former pet, or a place that had been special were amazing blessings for the participants. There was laughter and tears as partners exchanged information. The afternoon ended and people left to get dinner. Most participants had signed up for a mini session that evening. Anna and Suzanne both wanted to learn more about reincarnation.

Dinner was juicy burgers and sweet potato fries at a place close to the hotel that Amber found. Lily was having dinner with her mother, but Anna and Suzanne joined Amber.

"This afternoon was the best thing so far," said Amber. "I saw a golf club. That was it, but it was enough, because my partner started crying when I told her what I saw in my mind's eye. She told me her deceased father had been an avid golfer."

"It is easier for me to receive messages from the deceased than angels," said Suzanne, "I'm always so surprised when the picture I get in my head actually has meaning for the person."

"I know what you mean. All I saw was a frozen pond, and my partner knew her deceased cousin was with us. Her cousin had a pond that the two skated on every winter when they were young. My partner knew immediately who was with us when I told her what I saw," said Anna.

"I am really tired, but I want to learn about crystals. You both signed up for reincarnation, right? I heard that the lady teaching actually does past-life regressions. I might do that sometime," said Amber.

"I want to learn more about reincarnation, but I'm not interested in trying a past life regression. It doesn't matter to me who I was before this life, nor if I even had a previous life. I just like hearing the stories," said Anna.

"I've read a little about it. Lots of people around the world believe in it. I read stories about young children knowing foreign languages and names of people and places that couldn't be explained," said Suzanne.

"Those are the kind of things I want to hear," said Anna.

The evening did not disappoint the girls. The girls learned new things and met even more people. It was a night when one feels overwhelmed with the mysteries of life but is glad that there are people who can help explain some of the complexities.

Chapter 17

Sunday morning began with fresh fruit, eggs, and muffins. What Anna really wanted was a chocolate donut, but donuts weren't on the buffet. The morning conversation was upbeat. After breakfast, everyone gathered for their last couple hours together. Anna and Suzanne sat with a group of teenagers they had met the night before. Mary began with answering the questions that people had written the day before.

"Many of you have asked questions about establishing a meditation area in your homes. I believe everyone needs their own space. It can be bedroom corner, a chair by your garden, any place you can be by yourself. Much has been written about the use of candles, crystals, incense, prayer beads, and even flowers in creating a worship area. My suggestion is this: you need whatever you think you need. If lighting candles, using prayer beads, and burning incense helps you meditate then do it. I believe God only wants to hear our voices and doesn't care what we do to quiet ourselves in order to pray and listen.

"What I find fascinating is how similar worship rituals are among various religions. Prayer beads, candles, flowers, and music and dance are all a part of worship. And the reason we are here today—the belief in angels—is shared by many religions.

"I know many of you brought angel cards with you, so now is the time you get to use them. I'll lead you in a meditation, and then you can get with a partner and use your cards. Stephanie and I will be available to answer questions. There are several people in the room who have used cards for years; those people will also be available to help. Let's begin."

Anna enjoyed using her cards, and she and the other teens stayed together reading to each other. There was laughter and some thoughtful moments when a person would realize the significance of the message she was receiving. There were always questions about boyfriends and what the future might hold. Any time the romance card appeared, there was a joyful outburst.

The teens at the workshop had bonded, and many planned to keep in touch. Girls had attended for a variety of reasons, and all had found at least one thing to take with them. Having people of all ages and backgrounds coming together to discuss angels had an enormous impact on the girls. Spending a weekend talking about angels certainly proved beneficial.

The morning went quickly and ended with Mary thanking everyone for attending; she encouraged everyone to remember to find time to feed their spiritual selves. As they left, everyone received an angel pen. Mary said she hoped that the women would carry the pens in their purses, and when they pulled it out to write, they'd be reminded that their angels were with them.

Mary thanked Anna and Suzanne for being at the workshop and wanted to hear their thoughts about the weekend. They suggested a workshop for teens and a teen corner as part of Mary's website. When asked if they wanted to help with these things, both girls said yes.

Anna's dad was waiting in the lobby for the girls, and Mark was with him.

"Hey, what are you doing here?" Anna asked, looking at Mark.

"Oh, we came early so I could see some of my friends. I met them at the mall and hung out for a while," Mark answered, looking towards Suzanne.

"What did you do, Dad?" asked Anna as he took her bag.

"I brought my laptop and got some work done. Now I have time to spend with my favorite daughter," Dave said with a laugh. "So, how was it?"

"It was great, Dad, really great. Thanks for coming to get us."

"You're welcome. I'm glad you had a good time. I hear your brother is doing better," Dave said to Suzanne.

"Yes, I talked to my parents this morning, and they think he'll be able to come home from the hospital by the end of the week. He just needs to keep improving."

"Your mom sounded optimistic when I talked to her last night. Was the workshop all you had hoped it would be, Suzanne?"

"That and more."

"I'm glad. Let's head home if you have everything."

Mark and Dave didn't ask any more questions about the workshop. Knowing that the girls had a good time was enough. They talked about the Buckeye's spring game coming up and the weight training Mark was doing for his football program.

Suzanne and Anna sat quietly reviewing the weekend's activities. Both were surprised when Mark turned around and told Anna that Maddie had called him.

"She wanted to know what you were doing over break. I told her you were at an angel workshop."

"Oh, great. I'm sure she had a comment about that."

"No, she didn't say anything other than she hoped I could help get you two back together. She said she missed you, and that last year you had gone to Florida with her and her family on spring break. Being there without you this year was very difficult for her. She did seem sad, Anna."

"Mark, Maddie just wanted to talk to you. She has my number on her speed dial. She could have texted me if she wanted me. She wanted to talk to you." Anna felt like she was explaining something to a small child. *Men are so dense!* she thought.

"Well, maybe. She did ask if I'd meet her at the coffee shop so she could talk to me about you."

"Oh, brother! And what did you say?"

"I told her she should talk to you; that I didn't want to get into the middle of anything."

"And then?"

"She cried and said I was insensitive and that the real reason I wouldn't see her was because I was interested in someone else."

"What did you say to that?" Anna was very eager to hear his answer.

"I told her she was right, and then we hung up." As Mark answered Anna's question, he looked in Suzanne's direction.

Anna smiled broadly and said, "I doubt if you'll hear from Maddie again after telling her that. I'll see Maddie tomorrow at school, and maybe we'll talk."

"I can't imagine you and Maddie not being together. Like Grandma said, 'You can't have peanut butter without jelly,'" Anna's dad said, wanting to discuss this with her.

"Dad, I loved how Grandma said that about us, but tastes change and so do relationships. So many things have happened this year, and we have gone in different directions. I still plan on being Maddie's friend, but we won't ever be like we were." Anna wanted to add that adults get divorced and this wasn't that different.

Chapter 18

"Hey, Anna, wait up!" shouted Mark down the crowded school hallway, and he hurried to catch up with her. "Did your dad tell you about the fire pit we're going to build down by the creek?"

"Yes, he told me about it last night. We can finally roast hot dogs down there," said Anna smiling as she readjusted her load of books.

"Only if you can help. Dave told me to get a work crew together for next weekend. I thought we'd ask Thom, Kevin, and Matt."

"Kevin?" Anna asked surprised.

"Yeah, he knows I like Suzanne, but he is after Maddie now. She told him she was still mourning me, but she is considering going out with him. I swear that girl is always acting," Mark said, shaking his head.

"I'm supposed to work next Saturday, but I'll see what I can do. The bell's going to ring. I'll talk to you later," Anna said before rushing to homeroom.

Anna found Maddie at lunch. Her tan made her even more gorgeous. She talked happily about the beach and the awesome rays, and only asked what Anna had done over break when the bell rang. Anna told her she'd worked and gone to Cincinnati for the weekend. She didn't mention why, but of course Maddie already knew. Neither girl mentioned Mark, nor did Maddie say that she had missed not having Anna with her in Florida.

The workshop had certainly affected Anna, because when she returned to school, she felt like a different person. She couldn't explain the difference, but it was there. Suzanne and Anna were developing a close friendship, but she still missed Maddie. She knew they would continue to speak to each other, but eating lunch together every day and talking on the phone every night was a thing of the past. They both needed something else and were finding it in other friends. Losing Maddie's friendship was more painful than breaking up with her former boyfriend, Ross.

The next day, Suzanne and Anna ate lunch with girls who knew Anna and Suzanne had attended Mary's angel workshop in Cincinnati. The girls were eager to hear all about it.

"I'll have everyone over to my house on Friday, so you can tell us everything," offered Marissa as six girls sat around a lunchroom table. She had been at Mary's workshop in Sweet Grove and was a good friend of Suzanne's.

Most of the girls said they could come but didn't want to wait until Friday to hear what happened at the workshop.

"Just tell us a few things every day. You know, like teasers, and then the show will be on Friday," suggested Emma enthusiastically.

Anna laughed. She really did feel close to her new friends. They were excited just like she had been to hear her mother's stories. She jokingly began, "Once upon a time in a faraway land called Cincinnati..." The girls all laughed and then quieted down to listen.

"I liked the stories of people who had visits from deceased loved ones. A woman whose husband died of cancer told of her experience. She and her husband had agreed that after he passed, he would show her that he was still with her by moving some picture that hung on their wall. Well, the man died, and his mother stayed with her daughter- in-law a few days after the funeral. The woman was missing her husband terribly and kept looking at the picture to see if it had been moved. Finally, she said to her mother-in-law, 'Have you noticed this picture being crooked?' The mother-in-law answered, 'Have I?! I've been straightening it for the last two days.' There are so many stories I want to share; I know I'll have to write them down or I'll forget. Suzanne knows a lot too."

The bell rang and signaled it was time to go back to work. Spring break was now a thing of the past, and teachers were describing the numerous end of the projects they so loved to assign.

Thom walked Anna to her locker at the end of the day but didn't have time to talk. He had baseball practice and said he'd call later. He'd already told Mark he'd help build the fire pit on Saturday, so that took care of their Saturday night plans. The helpers were being paid with food, and knowing Anna's dad, that meant steaks. *Maybe Lauren could make her gourmet potatoes. Oh, a banana cream pie would be a great dessert, and everybody likes that. I am starving! I really need to eat more at lunch. An apple and a cup of yogurt is not enough,* Anna decided.

Anna was taking her time getting her things from her locker when she heard books hitting the floor and a locker being slammed shut. She looked towards the sound and saw a girl struggling to pick everything up. Closing her locker she went to help the girl.

"Hi, can I help?"

A pair of teary blue eyes looked up at Anna and then immediately looked down. "It's okay; I got it," muttered the girl.

Anna had already begun gathering the notebooks and folders. "You must be a walker like I am. I've got time to help. I'm glad I don't have to rush to catch a bus. It's nice not to have to hurry after a long day. I'm Anna," she said, standing.

"I know who you are. You're the angel girl," said the girl without looking at Anna.

"No, I'm just Anna. Here's your stuff."

"Thanks, I'm Kelly," she said, trying to get her things together. Black streams of eyeliner etched her checks, and her nose was beginning to drip. "Do you have a tissue? I seem to be falling apart."

"Let me check. Yep, here's one," Anna said, getting it from her purse and handing it to Kelly. Anna didn't know what to say, but she didn't think she should just leave.

"I heard you were nice. I think I'm okay now. You don't have to stay and babysit me," Kelly said awkwardly.

"I walk towards First Avenue. I wouldn't mind some company if that's the way you're headed," said Anna, wondering what was going on with this girl.

Kelly hesitated and then accepted the offer. The conversation was slow at first, but by the time they reached the library, they had begun to feel more at ease with each other. Since it was a warm spring day, they decided to sit by the fountain and breathe in the sun and fresh spring air.

"The sun sure feels good," Kelly said as she threw her head back so her face could feel the warmth. "I'm better now. Don't feel like you have to stay with me."

"I'm enjoying the sun too. Are you a sophomore?"

"Yes, and I just turned sixteen. I need to get a job. The guidance counselor thought he had some leads, but everything is filled. I hate to go home and tell mom there's still nothing. That's why I was so upset; I saw Mr. Frank last period. My mom's hours were cut back at her job, and I have to find something. It's always been a struggle at our house, but now things will be worse. My mom doesn't handle change very well, so her being home extra hours will only give her more time to drink. Sometimes I get tired of taking care of her," Kelly said, shaking her head like a defeated child. "I'm sure you didn't plan on listening to some sob story. I think my guardian angels must have sent you. That's why I'm telling you all this."

"Your angels?" asked Anna.

"Uh huh, I sort of have been praying lately, and I asked for someone to help me. I heard about you and all the angel stuff, so I thought I'd give it a try. My mom and I used to go to church, but after my dad left, we stopped. We pretty much stopped everything. Anyway, I asked God to tell my angels that I could use some help. I thought the guidance counselor would provide the help, but he hasn't yet! Now I think you were sent." Kelly looked at Anna, clearly wanting affirmation that Anna was the answer to Kelly's prayers.

"My grandma always said there is no such thing as a coincidence. So maybe you're right. Having someone to talk too is a help, I think. My mom owns a flower shop and knows a lot of business owners. There is always a big turnover in teen help, so maybe she'll know of an opening somewhere. I'll ask and give you a call."

The girls talked for a while, exchanged phone numbers, and headed home. As Anna walked down her street, she thought about Kelly and how she just happened to be in the hall when Kelly needed someone. *Those angels! They're really something!* Anna's stomach grabbed her attention, and her thinking switched to food. *I hope there are Girl Scout cookies still in the cupboard. I'm so hungry!*